SPINE-CHILLERS 2021

FROM THE SHADOWS

Edited By Allie Jones

First published in Great Britain in 2021 by:

Young Writers
Remus House
Coltsfoot Drive
Peterborough
PE2 9BF
Telephone: 01733 890066
Website: www.youngwriters.co.uk

Printed and bound in the UK by BookPrintingUK
Website: www.bookprintinguk.com
YB0484P

FOREWORD

Enter, Reader, if you dare...

For as long as there have been stories there have been ghost stories. Writers have been trying scare their readers for centuries using just the power of their imagination. For Young Writers' latest competition Spine-Chillers we asked pupils to come up with their own spooky tales, but with the tricky twist of using just 100 words!

They rose to the challenge magnificently and this resulting collection of haunting tales will certainly give you the creeps! From friendly ghosts and Halloween adventures to the gruesome and macabre, the young writers in this anthology showcase their creative writing talents.

Here at Young Writers our aim is to encourage creativity and to inspire a love of the written word, so it's great to get such an amazing response, with some absolutely fantastic stories.

I'd like to congratulate all the young authors in this collection - I hope this inspires them to continue with their creative writing. And who knows, maybe we'll be seeing their names alongside Stephen King on the best seller lists in the future...

CONTENTS

Skipton Girls' High School, Skipton

Holly Cornish (12)	59
Cara Shutt (12)	60
Fiza Ashraf (12)	61
Isabelle Murray (12)	62
Bella Zhang (12)	63
Abigail Cunliffe (12)	64
Lydia Noland (12)	65
Zahrah Siddique (12)	66
Chloe Dias (12)	67
Orla Clossick (12)	68

The Bourne Academy, Bournemouth

Maja Michalak (13)	69
Ellie Warren-Ross (12)	70
Ruben Molloy (12)	71
Connor Johnson (11)	72
Lily-Anne White (12)	73
Tayler Rees (12)	74
Isabel Mas-Barrett (13)	75
Megan Fuller (13)	76
Aliz Kadar (13)	77
Daisy-Mae Morgan (12)	78
Aaran Nickless (12)	79
Chloe Batcock (12)	80
Katie Booker (13)	81
Mollie Westerby (12)	82
Emily Bartlett (12)	83
Liam Bashford (12)	84
Joshua Douglas (12)	85
Charlie Spetch (13)	86
Olivia Tapping (12)	87
Miguel Marques (12)	88
Evie Clark (12)	89
Mya John-Charles (13)	90
Autumn Hall (13)	91
Alexis Wilkshire (13)	92
Ruben Harrison (12)	93
Liam Dawson-Deacon (12)	94
Aiden Blowers (12)	95

Kira Patel (12)	96
Ella Wilson (13)	97
Skye Goldsack (13)	98
George Robson (12)	99
Danielle Illsley (13)	100
Lacy Murphy (13)	101
Edward Isaacs (12)	102
Liam Dewet (12)	103
Emily Hall (12)	104
Eloise Martin (12)	105
Effy Altun (11)	106
Riley Snell (13)	107
Oliver Kieltyka (12)	108
Jasmin Morris (12)	109
Laila Ashour (11)	110
Maria Deka (13)	111
Isla Maher (12)	112
David Daniels (12)	113
Aaron Clark (12)	114
Matthew Sholto-Douglas-Vernon (12)	115
Olivia Martin (12)	116
Josh Marshall (13)	117
Ryan Hartwell (13)	118
Ruby Long (12)	119
Phoebe Palmer (12)	120
Lexie Cliffe (13)	121
Holly Carley-Lamb (12)	122
Jaydn Hardy (12)	123
Chelsea Johnston (12)	124
Jayden Rodger (12)	125
Tia-Louise Tuck (2)	126
Michael Farrow (13)	127
Teyla Cave (12)	128
Sophie Hill (12)	129
K Green (13)	130
Liberty Bond (13)	131
Ella-Grace Tyrrell (13)	132
Jensen Fox (12)	133
Kain Dix (13)	134
Chloe Calvert (11)	135
Lujin Houari (12)	136
Alex Sherring (12)	137

Sophie Mandley (12)	138
Lorelei Houson (13)	139
Lily Hillier (12)	140
Amelia Catmull (12)	141
Imogen Roach (12)	142
Logan McDonnell (13)	143
Alisha Culwick (12)	144
Aysha Roberts (13)	145
Emily Li (11)	146
Veda Maqsudi (12)	147
Brooke Dunning (12)	148
Natasha Daniels (12)	149
Enya Weir (12)	150
Sky Stratton (12)	151
Jasmine Wright (12)	152
Inayat Begum-Singleton (12)	153
Maisie-Mae Irvine (12)	154
Lukas Bailey (13)	155
Iliana Bevan (12)	156
Elizabeth Liberty (12)	157
Alex Harris (12)	158
Mia Dillon (12)	159
Ethan Searley (12)	160
Marc Dediu (12)	161
Daniel Gilbert (12)	162
Stephanie Howard (12)	163
Isobel Golding (12)	164
Daniel Drury-Wright (12)	165
Emily Soady (12)	166
Oliver Pollitt (13)	167
Ella Somers (12)	168
Oliver Bartlett (12)	169
Sophie-Mae Chick (12)	170
Ella Bullen (13)	171
Jack Smith (12)	172
Callum Casserley-Pyne (12)	173
Cameron Dillon (12)	174
Courtney Arnold (12)	175
Lewis Philogene-Jones (12)	176
Shorinne Davis (12)	177
Letisha Lillington (12)	178
Jamie Dean (12)	179
Fynnley Youngs (12)	180

Jake Gostling (12)	181
Maya Punal (12)	182
Dania Hamadi (11)	183
Alfie Messom (13)	184
Max Perkins (13)	185
Logan Reddick (13)	186
Alexander Wakefield (13)	187
Jake Carr (13)	188

Venn Boulevard Centre, Kingston Upon Hull

Harvey Whitehead (12)	189
Layla Kirk (12)	190

Westbourne School, Sheffield

Jennifer Himan (12)	191
Bethany Rowson (12)	192
Joshua Gilbert (12)	193
Elena Larkin (12)	194
Rui Seymour (11)	195
Isabella Spencer (11)	196
Poppy Fletcher (12)	197
Leo Reed (12)	198
George Blank (11)	199
Matilda White (12)	200
Anton Singleton (12)	201
Samuel Peters (12)	202
Harry Carter (12)	203
Harry Johnstone (12)	204
Charlie Jackson (12)	205

THE MINI SAGAS

UNDERCOVER

Blue lights and the deafening sound of screaming sirens flooded my ears. Another policewoman approached me and stood there, shaking her head, defeated. "It's awful, isn't it? I've never witnessed a murder as brutal as this one." I nodded and nervously shuffled my feet. The cold puddle reflected our pale faces and then the policewoman took something out of her pocket. In bold letters were the words 'CRIME SCENE, DO NOT CROSS'. "You better help me put this up before the detectives arrive." Suddenly, it became real. I glanced down at my fingernails. The bloodstains were still there.

Esther Beckingsale (12)
Bablake School, Coventry

ASSASSIN'S FAILURE

He was there. On the sofa watching TV. The lights flickered, off, on. He turned around, a frightened expression on his face. His eyes were placed where I stood before. He turned back to the TV. My sharpened knives raised. "Argh!" his dagger was in hand. I fell. His eyes looked down on me. He smirked as he said, "Try again!" in a deep tone, I saw the rest of his minions, the ones that escaped my blades. *Damn!* I thought. *He was prepared!*
"You... Just started, a war!" he called. A white face behind him. I smiled. "Ha!" *Thud!*

Jeevan Bains (12)
Bablake School, Coventry

THE HAUNTED

I could hear voices from inside. Faint whispers echoed around the abandoned house. The floorboards creaked as you stood on them, alerting them that they were being watched. Light rays, illuminating the room, made it enough light to see the light reflecting off the ghost. It tried to pull me to the black hole. "Nooo!" I screamed, reaching for the wall. Whilst resisting, I slipped, falling onto the concrete floor. The knife was now closer than ever before. A shiver shot down my spine. Fumbling, I grabbed a knife but my frail arms just couldn't reach her. It was useless.

Eben Jarratt (12)
Bablake School, Coventry

THE DRAGON OF THE FOREST

In the dapped light of the ferocious forest, there stood a mysterious creature whom no one knew. Except for one person. Me. Every morning, I walked past the forest and caught glimpses of this chaotic creature. Today, however, was different. I saw the whole beast. It was a dragon. Not any fairy-tale, ordinary dragon. It was jet-black with serpentine, slate scales. It stopped rustling the emerald bushes around it. There was stillness. It opened its mouth, rich red blood came pouring out. Flames of vermillion and so many shades of orange came flashing out of its mouth. It was fire!

Anand Kaur Bharath (12)
Bablake School, Coventry

HAUNTED

Trembling with fear, I walked down the stairs. *Screech!* I haltered to a stop. Scared. Once I'd stepped on the floor, violins, pianos and flutes started to sing and dance. Creatures were crawling through pictures, ghosts were flying through walls. Something touched me. Frozen. I couldn't move. My heart was moving faster than ever. I was possessed! Then all of the creatures created a formation. It was an arrow pointing to something. The creature turned me around. I saw it. My soul sank. It was the Devil pointing a spear on fire at me. Was this the last of me?

Amar Krajisnik (12)

Bablake School, Coventry

CAMPING

In the deep dark forest sits an abandoned log cabin. The windows smashed. Everything about the cabin was terrifying but one day a group of teenagers were on a camping trip, foolishly they set up camp near the cabin and decided to start a campfire. Little did they know that secretly, there was a killer in the woods. Suddenly, they heard a twig snap and thought, *it must have been an animal.* Out of nowhere they heard a scream and realised their friend had been snatched by someone. Tension and fear were slowly building in the air. Silence, pure silence.

Charles Kinson (11)
Bablake School, Coventry

CIRCLES, SQUARES AND TRIANGLES

It was 8pm. I had put the kid to bed and I was watching TV. *Buzz!* The TV flickered. "Circles, squares and triangles, go and check on the child." My heart skipped a beat, I nervously went to check on the child. They were sleeping soundly in their bed. I started creeping down the stairs until the phone started ringing. I picked it up. "Circles, squares and triangles, go and check on the child..." This time it was louder, I went back upstairs and opened the door. There it was, a cold body cut up into circles, squares and triangles.

Lily Harris (12)
Bablake School, Coventry

ESCAPE?

As I turned around the street corner into a darkness engulfed alleyway, I could hear his footsteps thudding down the cracked concrete pavement. I cowered behind a bin, this was the only protection I could find. To me, this was a fortress. He was calling to me saying that if I came out, I would be spared. "This would never happen," I whispered to myself. The silence wasn't right, every noise was a comfort. A cloak of silence had been thrown over the alley. Behind me, my pursuer had caught up with me. A glint of metal pierced my eyes...

James Hayselden (12)
Bablake School, Coventry

MIRROR, MIRROR, ON THE WALL

Eyes filled my small dark room, screams and screeches flooded around my ears as I frantically turned round in horror. I clutched my bed quilt and pulled it up to my trembling lips. The cold air blew through my long hair as I stared at my reflection in the mirror. I hid. The shadows were everywhere. The walls turned darker than they were before. A knock, and another. My mirror felt like it was snapping. The fear built up inside me. I heard shattering from inside the shadowed glass. The door creaked open. There it was, my blood-dripping reflection.

Olivia Bolstridge (12)
Bablake School, Coventry

HEAVEN AND HELL

Thunder showed danger, lightning showed fear yet the grass still danced melancholy to the melody the wind sang. Her nails left marks on my arm. I slithered away from the darkness only to be pulled back in. I kicked. I screamed, her nails grew deeper into my skin, tickling my bone. The knife glistened in the darkness leaving a poisonous trail. A smirk crawled across my face. Ash filled the sky. Her ash. Free cremation for her except there is no priest, no Heaven, no rest. Just Satan and her new home, hell. Bit by bit, the world was restored.

James Davies (12)
Bablake School, Coventry

ASSASINATION

It was midnight. He was tossing and turning in his bed trying to get to sleep. Then he realised he was sweating. *I must've had too much caffeine*, he thought as he got out of bed and looked out into the night. All of a sudden, he heard a creak. He shot out of bed and slowly crept into the silent landing. The lights suddenly turned on, and he heard another creak. He cautiously crept down the stairs and into the living room. That was when he saw it. The black figure emerged from the shadows. "Got you," he said.

Ethan Doidge (12)
Bablake School, Coventry

FRIEND OR FOE?

My hand was clutching the knife in my pocket, waiting, for something, anything a noise, a sound, something to reassure me I was still alive. The red lamp shone down, the room dry and hot, like a desert during a drought. The flaking white paint shone deep red in the light, a shadow of a once-loved bedroom. A mirror in the corner of the room slouched against the wall, covered in cobwebs and thick with a layer of dust. Screeching downstairs, like nails on a chalkboard. But the door was locked, and the windows closed. I was not alone.

Michael Masterson (12)
Bablake School, Coventry

THEY'RE WATCHING

I could feel eyes on me from every direction. Goosebumps grazed my arms as I left my bed for the cold, dark unknown to explore. Searching through the void under my bed, I found nothing but a striped sock. Venturing over to my wardrobe, I opened the doors and felt a cold chill on my spine, but nothing. I felt the breeze get stronger and my bones started to rattle in my flesh. I felt drawn to the window, almost as if I were summoned there. I tore the curtains apart, then I saw it. All 10 feet of it...

Amba Bodali-Bosson (11)
Bablake School, Coventry

DOWNPOUR

Lightning cracked as it pierced the charcoal clouds. The thunderous rain crashed onto the lush jungle, while Elden made his way inside the decrepit building nestled within the thick undergrowth. The periodic clicks echoed throughout the damp hallways. Suddenly, blood-curdling growls and shrieks shattered the atmosphere. The downpour continued to crash onto the jungle canopy. Elden burst into the nearest room, guided by fright. Unknown to him, it was in there. The bloodstained shadow turned viciously, flesh in its jaw. Elden fled in terror, but another awaited him in the hallway, as the rain continued to crash onto the canopy.

Cai Harris (15)
Cwmtawe Community School, Pontardawe

THE ABANDONED MENTAL HOSPITAL

"Go on... press it." The darkness was creeping closer. "See what happens!" All the rust and dirt was intimidating me. But I did press the button eventually. The silence was uncomfortable until... The sound of a terrifying fire alarm. We felt different like we were about to die. I felt a breeze, not just any type of breeze, a damp breeze. The mist was crawling towards us. "Kay?"

"I'm here."

We couldn't see anything anymore, walking through the abandoned hospital to find the exit. "I feel weird. Like something is creeping up behind me." I turned around...

Katie Furnish (12)

Cwmtawe Community School, Pontardawe

THE HORROR IN THE BEAUTY

Terrifying rumours struck fear into the wary village. Rumours about the disappearances of young adults. Witnesses claimed that they had seen fairly attractive creatures that were half-human, half-fish. At midnight, these creatures would sing, luring their unfortunate victims to the castle cliffs nearby. These victims were in a trance until it was too late. The rumours could not be proved true and the disappearances went on. However, the cliffs nearby had been stained red, like a reminder that the mysterious killers were real and were always nearby. Nobody was ever caught, allowing the killers to continue their crimes.

Lacey Evans (15)
Cwmtawe Community School, Pontardawe

UNWANTED

Darkness. A cackling laugh was heard from a distance. The tall, decrepit stairs looked down upon them. The food fell. The cackling laugh got closer and closer until suddenly, it stopped. They felt the presence of this unwanted spirit. Their minds went blank, whether to run or stay. The presence left. Cold air blew, shivers down the spine. Then *bang!* The sound of a large tall body tumbling down the stairs. But, nothing there. The presence appeared again. Petrified, they stood there, nowhere to run. Just darkness. A sudden whisper, "Here I am, boo!" Turned quickly in fear, and there...

Caoimhe Hancock (15)
Cwmtawe Community School, Pontardawe

THE ABANDONED HOSPITAL

It just struck midnight, Liz, Beck, and Emily were all wandering around the abandoned hospital. All of a sudden, Emily was nowhere to be seen. Liz and Beck screamed, "Emily!"

Emily screamed, "Help me!" Her voice echoed.

Liz left Beck to find Emily. Liz came back and said, "She is dead". Beck ran away. Liz heard a voice saying, "Time to die." Liz cried "Where are they?"

"That's for me to know and you to find out." Liz ran to find Beck, he was dead. Soon after, Liz died covered in blood and knife wounds.

Ffion Thomas (12)
Cwmtawe Community School, Pontardawe

THE WOMAN

I can't sleep. I toss, I turn, I tumble and twirl around the messy bed, her presence keeping me up. She mourns, crying tears darker than oil. Her dark brown hair tangles around her damaged and decrepit body. The sobs, like heckles, silence my thoughts as she screams for her dead child whom she begs to see again. Begging to bring them back. Eventually, after she stops, a gunshot rings out, forcing me awake. I look around, scared and frightened. The sun illuminates the room, the door opens, the woman stands there smiling. She opens her mouth, "Good morning sweetie!"

Vivienne Evans (15)
Cwmtawe Community School, Pontardawe

AN ABYSS OF BLACK PETALS

The night was starless but the ghostly outline of the abandoned prison could be seen on top of the cliff, towering above the vast black abyss below it. Cleo ascended up the side of the cliff, torch in hand, her blackish hair flying in the wind that was pushing against her. An eerie sound pierced the air. "Who's there?" No reply. When Cleo got to the top, she stopped, caught her breath, and walked over to the edge of the cliff. "You will be revived!" Black petals fell from her hand into the abyss. The noise struck again. "Wait, no!"

Nyla Oduro-Sarfo (12)
Cwmtawe Community School, Pontardawe

THE LONELY SPIRIT

The fog grew as darkness progressed. The church bells rang and the spirits arose. Footsteps grew louder and louder until suddenly, they stopped. I felt as if someone was watching me. Their presence made me uncomfortable. I felt breathing on my neck. My eyes scanned around the dark room but no one was there. My heart began to beat rapidly and adrenaline rushed through my veins. *Bang!* A book flew across the room, but I thought that I was alone. My eyes searched the room once more, this time I saw a tall figure behind me. "Get out," it said...

Amber Hulse (15)
Cwmtawe Community School, Pontardawe

BREAK-IN!

The sharp shine of the knife glinted at me. As I stood there quivering I thought of all the things that had brought me here. I'd been left alone, unsupervised. I heard the front door slam open. *Bang!* As I gingerly stepped closer towards the door, a few thoughts crossed my mind. One: why did they leave me alone? Two: people really need to start locking their doors. Three: the way the door slammed shut, he's probably alerted someone nearby. I hoped I was right. Someone needed to stop me. One last step... I'm ready to claim my first victim!

Olivia Minshall (14)
Cwmtawe Community School, Pontardawe

THE SCHOOL

The corridors were pitch-black. No windows, no lights, just my phone flashlight. One more hour till the first member of staff arrived. I couldn't phone anyone as I had no data. The sound of rats on the ceiling tiles messed with my mind. Suddenly, a terrifying thud behind me followed by a creepy laugh. My heart sank. With terror and fear, heavy footsteps began to walk, then run. Sprinting towards me, I looked behind me to see bright red eyes coming closer, closer and closer, followed by the footsteps. Then a cold, wrinkly hand grabbed me...

Owain Jason (13)
Cwmtawe Community School, Pontardawe

THE CASTLE

A group of friends decided they wanted to explore a castle that had been abandoned for years. Once they entered they split into two groups, one for the throne room and one for the armoury. One group had Tom and Jerry, the other had Reece and Jim. After they split, Tom and Jerry heard a shout and went to go look, they couldn't find Reece or Jim but what they did find was a huge shadow. They ran, with the shadow slowly following. They split to hide. After ten minutes Tom felt a hand touch his shoulder, he said "Jerry?"...

Callum Jenkins (12)
Cwmtawe Community School, Pontardawe

BEDTIME

I crawl up the stairs, the piercing sound of the traps screeching as I fall into my creased bed. As I let my horror thoughts take over. Dogs barking, feet thumping and babies crying outside whilst I'm trapped within the silent darkness. Parents out of town in the thunderous nightmare. Phone service down, nobody around. As I drift off the mind and spirit begin to play tricks with me. The door creaks open as the shuffling feet skim up to the side of my bed. I feel paralysed, I can only sit and let the spirit glare at my soul...

Joshua Sharville (15)
Cwmtawe Community School, Pontardawe

THE THING

The car rolled to a stop. Out of fuel. Tom stopped next to the forest. Tom wondered what to do next. The shadows almost seemed to move and turn. In the corner of Tom's eye, he saw something run. He glanced to see nothing. Then a growl from the other side of the car. In the trees, he saw a thing. He could only see a silhouette but it stood like a human and was tall and skinny, it had fingers the size of rulers. It roared and charged towards Tom. Scared, Tom quickly ran for his life. He tripped...

Daniel Jones (12)
Cwmtawe Community School, Pontardawe

MIDNIGHT

I woke up suddenly at midnight, it was pitch-black. It was silent. I looked around to find my phone, then all of a sudden I heard footsteps at the bottom of my stairs, loud creaking as if the stairs were on the edge of snapping like thin ice. I got out of there, I flicked the light switch and remembered the power was out. I grabbed a torch and looked down the stairs, no one was there. I slowly walked down the stairs, I then reached the bottom where I saw a bloody man and he was looking for me...

Adam Jones (15)
Cwmtawe Community School, Pontardawe

THE GHOST IN THE ABANDONED HOUSE

Go on, press it! The doorbell was very rusty, I pressed it. Everyone ran as fast as they possibly could. I hid behind some trees in the woods, we all were laughing at what we did at the time. The door opened, no one was laughing anymore. No one was there! We went inside it was very dark, *bang!* Something fell over as someone ran past us. We went to see what fell over. It was a bear's head! It was chopped off its own body. It smelled so bad, I turned around, my friends were gone!

Jakson Davey (11)
Cwmtawe Community School, Pontardawe

THE MIDNIGHT MURDER

I had my knife hid under my T-shirt. I had picked the lock on the door and got in. After a shiver and deep breath, I crept around the house, looking to see where he was. As silently as possible, I went up the stairs. My stomach was twisting, I knew there was no going back. I checked one room, nothing but darkness. I went into another one and sensed something in it, it was pitch-black though. The darkness took me in. Then I saw him, I raised my knife and brought it to his neck...

Corey-Jayden Sherlock (12)
Cwmtawe Community School, Pontardawe

THE HAUNTED MAN

One dark, gloomy night, I went to the funfair with my friend. I loved it there. That night, we had lots of fun, but then this happened: there was a man following us wherever we went. We walked down this spooky, scary, narrow alleyway which took us to my house. Suddenly, we heard a huge bang on the door and we knew it was him standing outside. My phone rang and this voice like an echo through the phone whispered, "Watch out, I am going to find you!"

Demi Lin (14)
Cwmtawe Community School, Pontardawe

TO THE DEPTHS

Thunder crackled fiercely into the water. My ship twisted and rocked, nearly capsizing. The waves were gigantic hands pushing me from side to side. I got my crew to follow the storm procedures, hoping lives would be intact. We readied the escape boats in case of a treacherous disaster. As we progressed to our destination, the storm worsened, our ship began taking multitudes of water. I swear, I heard scraping, though. A strong bolt of lightning hit our sails, we were trapped. In the distance, a colossal fin emerged, it headed towards us rapidly. Then, it dipped beneath our ship...

Nezar Al-Khurayke (12)
King's Leadership Academy Hawthornes, Bootle

DEATHSNARL'S TALE

A dark beast emerges from the shadows to stalk poor unknowing souls. This creature has fangs as sharp as razor blades, huge claws shredding anything they touch, arms that are so long they drag along the floor, and a hunchback with shredded skin on it that reeks of blood. Roars can be heard from miles away. Mimicking the cries and screams of children whose fates have been sealed. This beast eats its targets after killing them but it doesn't just kill its targets straight away, it scares them, horrifies them, the more fear the more tastier, so beware the Deathsnarl.

Harrison Dunne (12)

King's Leadership Academy Hawthornes, Bootle

FIVE NIGHTS AT FREDDY'S

It was my birthday one night in 1983, the day I died. It was my birthday party and my parents brought me to Freddy Fazbear's pizzeria that had animatronics. I was scared of them. I hid under the table with shivers down my spine, it felt like hours flew by but then my older brother and his friends dragged me out from under the table. I was crying and shaking. They put my head to the animatronic's jaw! I couldn't see because of the tears in my eyes. Then I opened them... *Snap!* Its jaw clenched my skull...

Grace Ross (12)
King's Leadership Academy Hawthornes, Bootle

THE LONELY HAND

As I stepped onto the desolate path I felt my soul slip away from my chest. The crooked trees gasped at my presence. I could hear someone stepping towards me. I ran. I felt like the trees were closing in on me and I was not moving at all. I tripped on a tree root. I was enclosed against the malicious trees. The footsteps kept getting closer and closer until I could hear someone breathing. All I saw was a lonely decaying hand. It pulled me underground. I knew I would never see the light of day again...

Alissia Foy (12)

King's Leadership Academy Hawthornes, Bootle

THE CABIN IN THE WOODS

I was lost in the forest and I was cold. I found an abandoned cabin, it looked old. I went in and it looked used but old. I went to the fire and I felt like I was being watched. I got my phone, no service. I was stuck here. Some books fell off the shelf. I was confused. The front door opened but no one was there. I hid in the bedroom. I was scared. It was dark. It felt like someone was there. I got dragged out of the house and someone screamed, "Stay out!"

Cole Mcardle (12)
King's Leadership Academy Hawthornes, Bootle

SEVEN DAYS BEFORE I DIE

It went quiet, I ran as quickly as a fox, the fog clung onto me as I screamed as fear spurted out of me. I escaped out of its grasps and went like lightning to hide. The fog slowly clung onto the handle and turned it. I was sweating, it felt like someone had poured warm ice cubes on me. I covered my mouth with my trembling fingers. The door had been burst open by the beast. It clutched onto my meatball head. Argh! Nothing could destroy this monster.

Denise O'Brien (12)
King's Leadership Academy Hawthornes, Bootle

ABANDONED

"We shouldn't be here."

"Shut up, we will be famous!"

"Keep your voice down, somebody will hear us."

Charlie strode ahead without a second thought, but Ben held back. The fog swirled in around them as they approached the dark church, ominously looming over them precariously while spiders scuttled around. Twigs snapping under their feet, their breath visible. *Smash!* A window shattered and muffled laughter came from inside the church. suddenly, bells started ringing from inside, then a single *bang* and the laughter and shouting turned into a shrill scream!

Oliver Eriksson (13)

Sir John Leman High School, Beccles

A LIFE FOR A LIFE

A flash of lightning. A crash of thunder. Echoing voices of the newly deceased. I knew I shouldn't have been there, but I couldn't resist the temptation of curiosity. But you know what they say: "Curiosity killed the cat". Well I was one unlucky feline.

Creeping through the neglected hallway, something sinister caught my eye: a shadow looming over a strangled corpse, its face twisted in raw pain. I shuddered. Inching away from the rotting flesh, I noticed the shadow gazing despairingly at the body. His body. This shadow was trapped and about to trade a life for a life...

Lucy Amara Addison (12)
Sir John Leman High School, Beccles

THE NIGHTMARE NEIGHBOUR

You stare up at it, towering over you, its crooked lifeless self, with silhouettes filling the stained-glass, broken windows. Mind racing. Stomach in knots. You venture towards the house. The moon-lit sky covering the raging storm. You open the dusty door. The flash of lightning strikes behind you, it crushes the path you took, leaving the only option to go in. Scared, you tiptoe in, the eerie atmosphere making your spine tingle, you dare to climb up the twisty, towering stairs. Paintings around you follow your every move. Then behind you, a cold, menacing hand touches your shoulder...

Poppy Goodwin (12)
Sir John Leman High School, Beccles

CURIOSITY KILLED THE CAT

The thunder boomed, they creaked the door open, "Look, I just don't want to go," a boy whined. He didn't protest any longer after receiving angry glares. Lightning filled the room scaring an animal, bringing their attention to... a rotten... half-eaten, rat corpse. Then there were heavy footsteps above them. They investigated. As they climbed, the wood screamed. But they stopped. Across the wall was blood and they saw a figure in the gap of the door. His eye pierced through their souls, he opened it, a chainsaw started. Well, as they say, curiosity killed the cat.

Katie Ray (14)

Sir John Leman High School, Beccles

WHAT LURKS IN THE DARK

Surrounded. Enclosed. Silenced. Stolen in the twilight. The darkness was all-encompassing, pressing in more and more as time slipped by. She had been swallowed, there was no way out, not any more. She had been warned, warned about them. She wasn't in a room, nor a building. Just a fold of dark and shadows. Footsteps. The loud click-clack of shoes against the floorboards, closer and closer. They had no trouble with the dark. Almost inhumanely so. Really, she wasn't sure if they were human at all. Silence again. They had arrived. They were here. It was time...

Olivia Grant (14)

Sir John Leman High School, Beccles

MY GHOST BROTHER

"Come back, Tom!" called Collin from outside, but it was my younger brother Isaac who went missing only yesterday inside this abandoned house. He was here, I felt it! Already creeping up the staircase even through my shoes, I felt the cobwebs brushing my ankles. I had finished the stairs, a door was facing me, like it was calling my name. The door when opening was like a horror film. I walked in, no sign of him, "Isaac, Isaac," I whispered, but something started to sing, then everything went black. I screamed, was it Isaac, my ghost brother?

Sammy Tipple (12)
Sir John Leman High School, Beccles

ONE HUNDRED DIFFERENT DOORS

Door 68. What's inside I see? A deceased person which looks like me. Door 72. Another secret hidden? All I see are pure stygian faces glaring at me. Door 49. Wonder what's in here? A black-eyed child gazing down in fear. Final door. Door one. Who's the grinning figure peeping around the corner? Nasty images, I could walk inside, what would really happen if I stepped inside? Would the monsters go and hide, or would they make me die? Well, this is just a story, it doesn't make any sense. Except the slender figure watching me write this nonsense.

Sophie Edwards (12)
Sir John Leman High School, Beccles

THE BODY

There she was. About to visit her husband she hadn't seen in months. Her hand reached the doorknob of the dark, sunless house. *Click!* She turned it. The heavy metal door opened. She trudged in. There stood the figure. Its long fingers reached out to her. She ran. Through the house, up the stairs into a room. All that was there was a bed. she edged closer only to see a lifeless body. Her husband. His eyes staring up at nothing. The footsteps came. The room went cold. The wind whistled. It advanced towards her. Then her heart stopped. Dead!

Emilia Widdison (12)
Sir John Leman High School, Beccles

ABANDONED HOUSE

It was time for the dog walk. It was a dark and gloomy night, but we set off hoping for the best. As the night went on, I noticed a house in the distance. As we drew closer I heard music, giving me a headache. Not knowing whether to enter, but having the dog for protection we entered. I could hear doors squeaking upstairs, getting slightly worried, not too worried to stop investigating though. Slowly, moving up the stairs just to check if anyone was there, there wasn't, now starting to panic, wondering how the music played, we left.

Cora Payne (12)
Sir John Leman High School, Beccles

DANGERS OF THE DEEP

We'd been hanging around the pier all day, the glorious sunshine beating down on our backs. But the security of the sun was slipping away as quickly as the people left the beach to go home. My friend and I were strolling along the empty promenade when the glimmering moonlit sea became so welcoming to us. I knew it was dangerous, but the thought of having a refreshing dip was overpowering my common sense. We slipped in, unaware of the horrors of the sea at night. Suddenly a scream shocked my ears like electrocution, where had my friend gone?

Emily Lowther (12)
Sir John Leman High School, Beccles

THE RACING STORM

Run. That was all that I could think of when I saw the emerging storm. Deathly black clouds locked away the sky, cold piercing rain fell, blinding lightning ripped through, deafening rumbles screamed in my ears. The only place to go was an old solitary building. My legs started to ache, fire burning through my flesh. My lungs craved for more air as I pushed myself through the thick muggy fog. The storm's stomach rumbled and shot a strike of lightning at me, the one that would end my life. Realising I was too late, I accepted my fate.

Libby Mayston (13)
Sir John Leman High School, Beccles

THE MAGIC WELL

"Go to the magic well," whispered the sinister voice. I knew I wasn't supposed to be here and that became apparent when I heard the wooden floor creaking as a silhouette approached the window. "Go to the magic well." I stumbled over to the back door in hopes of escaping but it was no use since I felt something grabbing me. Suddenly I awoke. Was this all a dream? No, right now I was in front of the magic well. I felt an unsettling presence when without warning I was transported to another world. How did I get here?

Phoebe Harrington (12)
Sir John Leman High School, Beccles

THE DARE

I tiptoed down the road, my hands already sweating as I drew closer. A shiver darted down my spine as my fingertips grazed the door handle. It was a silly dare, but my curious mind felt I should investigate some more. The darkness began to engulf me. I felt an eerie presence but chose to ignorantly ignore it. I squinted my eyes as my hand began to clutch the handle and slowly twist it. Regrets flooded me as I drew closer like a predator with its prey. My mouth dropped. A figure in black began to approach me. I screamed!

Maddison Dexter (12)
Sir John Leman High School, Beccles

THE WOLF'S CABIN

The whining wind pushed against the cabin, a knocking and scraping on the windows. The banging became louder and louder, suddenly the door was being kicked in, the shadow of a wolf, a werewolf, it was midnight and a very eerie full moon, then the ear-piercing howl came from the cabin door. I ran through to the bedroom at lightning speed, to find an emergency hiding spot or exit but there was nothing, hiding under the bed was no use, but it was a last resort. It finally ended, with a final blood-curdling howl, it left.

Alexander Roberts (14)
Sir John Leman High School, Beccles

TRUTH OR DARE?

I banged on the heavy doors, screaming at the top of my lungs, "Help!" Tears rolled down my cheeks. Why did I decide to play truth or dare at night? It was normally fun but this time it had gone too far. I heard rustling behind me. Not wanting to turn around I clenched my fists preparing myself for the worst. I shivered, the church was cold and dark. My heart thudded madly inside my chest when something fell near my feet. Intrigued, I slowly knelt down and screeched as an eyeball was staring back up at me...

Ettie Goodwin (12)

Sir John Leman High School, Beccles

THE TOMBSTONE

Walking past the church window, the pictures on it staring through me. It was night-time but the sky was white. There, in the corner of my eye, I saw it. Was it really him? My heart boomed inside me. I was almost paralysed with the thought of what he might do. I had to run. I was inside the church when I peered through the only clear window I could find. I caught sight of someone digging. I didn't know who, but they were spine-chillingly tall with a look of murder in their eyes. All of a sudden, darkness...

William Fisher (12)
Sir John Leman High School, Beccles

THE PECULIAR HOUSE

One beautiful morning, I was on a walk with my dog. As we were walking we saw a house in the distance. My dog was interested and began pulling me that way. It started to rain. By the time we got there, it was thundering. The door was unlocked and no one was home. Throughout the whole day, it was hailing and our only choice was to stay. It began to get dark, still, no one was home. We stayed the night, but we didn't know we'd wake up to this! Broken windows, handprints and... where had my dog gone?

Evie Holmes (12)
Sir John Leman High School, Beccles

ALONE AND AFRAID

It was night. It was time. Not a star in sight. An ancient grand church overshadowed him. Ben was ready. The stained-glass windows brought enough light for him to see. He ambled around the church shaking and cautious. He came to a halt, confused, petrified. A deafening howl came from the other side of the church. He went to run but the doors locked behind him. He had no choice but to investigate. He entered the room to find a child lying there unconscious. He was alone and afraid.

Ben Block (12)
Sir John Leman High School, Beccles

NO TIME

The wind howled all around the church. Something felt wrong, things were pulling at my feet, arms and hair, trying to trip me up. Screaming, crying, and echoing sounds was all I heard. Suddenly, I looked up and saw a man holding an axe. I ran as fast as my legs could carry me out of the church and around the graveyard. It wasn't fast enough. The next thing I knew, his axe was on my neck. "What will happen next?" I screamed. Someone just laughed at me...

Molly Fleming (12)
Sir John Leman High School, Beccles

THE FOREST OF ICE

It was a warm night. Me and my family went out for a stroll in the woods as normal. We were in the middle of the woods when I noticed a tall black-cloaked figure was following us. I immediately turned around to see my whole family encased in ice. Frozen, how? Something was breathing heavily over my shoulder. I turned slowly. The black figure looking down at me with its sea-blue eyes. I tried to run, it grabbed me with its razor-sharp claw-like hands. Cold as... ice.

Harry Sutton (12)
Sir John Leman High School, Beccles

WHAT WOULD IT TAKE?

It roamed the halls. Sharp as the night and prepared to bite. Soon it will find you. Loud stomps make the earthquake as the building behind starts to crumble. Try to run and try to hide. Do whatever it takes to survive! Why did you agree? You hate what you have seen. Your friends are slain, their heads covered in each other's blood and put up like trophies on a wall. And yet there is hope. You have the key and a slim chance of what it may take to escape.

Bailey Bishop (13)
Sir John Leman High School, Beccles

THE WOODS

"Jack, no! Papa Joe told us stories about this place."
As we stumbled through the endless forest we heard a demonic scream that made a colossal crack in the silence of this horrifying place. I checked my pockets for a torch when I heard a bush shake, I looked up, where was Jack? I immediately ran, I was an ant trapped in a glass cup and I heard another deafening scream. There was just a sea of darkness and fear...

Tom Fiddes (12)
Sir John Leman High School, Beccles

THE DEAD ASYLUM

"Nikki!" His voice rang out, the asylum was empty. So noise echoed loudly. "I think we should go back."

"Don't be so scared, Evans. It can't be that bad, plus it's our job to investigate here."

"Fine, but this place is giving me the creeps." He stopped. "Woah, what's this?" He sounded disgusted.

"What did you see? I swear if-" She paused. Where was he? As she turned around she noticed something strange, there was a doll, black hair, black eyes. Dressed in black. "Evans?" she said nervously.

"He can't save you now." A voice laughed, and she just screamed!

Holly Cornish (12)
Skipton Girls' High School, Skipton

CANDLE IN THE WINDOW

The single candle flickered eerily in the mental asylum window. Lily's feet crunched over the bone-dry, brown grass. It might have been grass but she couldn't be sure. As she walked up to knock on the cracked wooden door, it creaked open eerily on its own. Lily stepped in warily and her eyes darted around. "Hello?" she asked.

"Hello," was the answer, but she hoped it was only an echo. Lily heard a scuffling from the entrance, she twisted around worriedly to see a hunched shadow. "Hello friend," said the shadowy figure. "Glad you could join me Lily..." he whispered.

Cara Shutt (12)
Skipton Girls' High School, Skipton

THE CIRCUS

Samuel walked through the wreckage, the memories crawling up his shoulders. He hadn't been in the circus for ages and it gave him a weird feeling as he walked over the stained floor. The windows and doors opened and closed rapidly as the wind howled, then the cannon wheeled towards him and what he saw changed everything because inside was his old manager, but not in one piece! Samuel couldn't believe what he was seeing. He thought he was hallucinating. Suddenly, he heard footsteps creeping up behind him, then an icy finger ran down his back, and Samuel just froze...

Fiza Ashraf (12)
Skipton Girls' High School, Skipton

IN THE DARK OF NIGHT

Silence. A child's bedroom smothered in darkness. The child awake in their bed. Night air breezed through the open window. That's how the shadows get in. They drift through, bringing a chilling coldness and a lurking sense of dread. The child senses their presence and tries to feign sleep. But the shadows are not fooled, not by the simple tricks of a naive child. They can tell the child is scared, they feed on the fear. The child succumbs. The shadows pick up the tiny, trembling body. They flee the bedroom as quickly and quietly as they came. Then, silence.

Isabelle Murray (12)
Skipton Girls' High School, Skipton

THE FUNFAIR

The place was empty, and the teacups that sat on the platform screeched as it spun on its rusty wheels. Everything was falling into pieces as time went on. I peeked my head around the corner and saw a man in all black, laughing and smirking at me. His stare went deep into me as I could feel a light thorny rope that enclosed around me, although nothing was there. The laughter and fun soon turned into crying and shrieking. My screams were silenced, dulling my senses and tightly wrapping me in a suffocating embrace. Everything went palely silent.

Bella Zhang (12)

Skipton Girls' High School, Skipton

THE ASYLUM OF SHADOWS

The group of untrained teenagers clambered over the wreckage of the asylum. Once they got inside, they headed to explore their first room. It was a room with a single bed, mirror and dresser. The wind whistled against stones on the building. Bea heard whispering in their ear. They felt their bodies being pulled away from them. The door slammed shut and locked. Adora turned towards Bea. That's when she saw. The figure grinning at everybody. She screamed for Bea to stop. It was useless. They were pulled into the mirror by the figures.

Abigail Cunliffe (12)
Skipton Girls' High School, Skipton

WHO RINGS THE BELL?

Bang!
"Officer Lockheart, was that you?"
The doors flung open. I heard footsteps so I ran in. I decided to investigate. I passed a few rooms that I suspected were once used as classrooms. I found myself in the hall. Old pictures from the 1800s, that were at a slanted angle, I also saw the old school bell. I wonder who used to be here and why it wasn't turned into something? I saw a figure in the window. A cold and sharp breath blew across my ear. The bell rang, the white figure was standing here, alone.

Lydia Noland (12)
Skipton Girls' High School, Skipton

THE FAIR WITH RIDES OF MYSTERY

In the foggy, abandoned fair, I walked deeper and deeper into the loss of fun and laughter. "What had happened here?" I asked myself. I saw all sorts of amazing rides, an abandoned Ferris wheel, a roller coaster that had worn out over the years. Obviously there were way too many things to say but it was a fun, scary, mysterious experience. But something felt wrong, very wrong. As if someone was here! Wasn't I the one who first discovered this place? I was sure I was and that all changed with a tap on my shoulder...

Zahrah Siddique (12)
Skipton Girls' High School, Skipton

ALIVE

Trembling in fear, I ran down the dark road, stones scattered everywhere. Long, bare trees stood up along either side and a gentle breeze was swirling down the highway. *Thud!* I spun around only to see a cat fall into a bin. But that didn't concern me because behind the bin was a graveyard, covered in vines. I slowly walked to a grave, leaning back on a tree that stood behind me. I felt something on my arm, and I turned my head slowly to realise there was a detached arm gripping my shoulder and it was moving...

Chloe Dias (12)
Skipton Girls' High School, Skipton

POLICE INTERROGATION: NELLY BLAKE

I really don't know what happened. I swear. I didn't push him. He fell. He fell off the school roof. I swear that's all I know. I don't know how he got there, apart from I led him up the stairs. I don't care that my fingerprints were on the knife, as long as you don't find it. You did? Oh well. I guess I'm lucky you didn't find the gun. I know you didn't. Why? Because it's in my pocket. You know, in case the best happens. I mean worst, I swear.

Orla Clossick (12)
Skipton Girls' High School, Skipton

THERE'S SOMEBODY UPSTAIRS

Sinisterly, floorboards creaked threateningly with every step. "We shouldn't have followed!" Beth muttered. Crows pecked on the windows. Almost a warning. Spiders crawled between their feet and smoke swirled around them.

"I only suggested, you followed," Ella rushed.

"What she said," Max whispered, not concerned.

The storm battered the windows, a ticking loudened as they neared a nauseating living room. Although they were in a group of three, entering the living room forced their minds into isolation.

Snap!

"Ow, my foot, my foot!" Beth screeched.

Creaking steps neared them. Both friends gripping Beth by her arms, couldn't get her out...

Maja Michalak (13)
The Bourne Academy, Bournemouth

WHITNEY

"I wonder if Whitney is here?" Ruby pulled out a Ouija board, while they sat in the church. Giggling, they asked if Whitney was there.

"Yes!"

Bang!

"Who was that?"

They turned around a doll was on the floor. "Are you Whitney?"

"Yes!"

The doors slammed shut and the candles blew out. The group stared at each other in the dark. Tiffany screamed! Something slapped her face. "How old are you Whitney?" asked Tiffany.

"15," said Whitney.

"Oh, the same age as us."

"Get out!"

The group ran out of the doors as fast as Usain Bolt...

Ellie Warren-Ross (12)

The Bourne Academy, Bournemouth

THE HOUSE OF MANY MIRRORS AND MORE

"Jake, don't do it!"

"Why not?"

"Hmm, why shouldn't you go in an abandoned mirror maze in an abandoned theme park?

"I'm going in Ben!"

I stepped in and suddenly an eerie mist grasped my ankles like an undead zombie! "Ben!" I shouted, fear racing up my spine. "I'm ready to come out now!" And that's when I saw it... A menacing clown chuckling behind me in the mirror. I shot around, there was nothing there! "Very funny Ben," I said but got no reply... All of a sudden, I heard a screech as a chill spiked my back. "Ben?"

Ruben Molloy (12)

The Bourne Academy, Bournemouth

THE HAUNTED HOUSE

"No Jess!" shouted Tom. "You can't go in there."

"I know," shouted Jess.

Tom's heart pounded against his chest as he saw Jess wrap her hands around the frozen, sharp door handle.

"Jess, don't go in!" shouted Tom.

She tiptoed in. "Hello," Jess shouted. "There is no one here, come in Tom." Suddenly, a dark figure pulled her away and she was never seen again.

100 years later, two children went into the house, Ana saw the dead body of Jess, seconds later a dark figure pulled them under the ground and they were never seen again.

Connor Johnson (11)

The Bourne Academy, Bournemouth

JACK, WHERE ARE YOU?

As the presence of someone's spirit towered over them, the chills leered Jack into the ancient church. Doors slammed, windows creaked and isolated candles flickered in the never-ending night. Trembling through the inescapable forest, the door threw itself open like it was inviting them in. Lurking through the medieval doorway, the bone-chilling aroma cornered them, like crocodiles to their prey. Menacingly, the door screamed like it had just been stabbed. Jack felt a bony, cold hand stroke his shoulder. Alfie slowly turned, he was gone... In shock, he sprinted away screeching, "Jack, where are you?"

Lily-Anne White (12)
The Bourne Academy, Bournemouth

STEPPING STONES

She was still jumping stone to stone. "Stop! It is not safe!" Lucy wasn't listening. I got more anxious for every step she took. "Lucy stop!"

"It's not gonna kill me or anything. Stop worrying!" Like that was going to help. The stones began to make sounds, they got louder for every step she took. "What's that noise Layla?" she said.

"I don't know, you should come back, if you take another step you could-" The ground began to shake, "Lucy! Run!" I yelled. She was gone. In a blink of an eye. The ground froze and all fell silent.

Tayler Rees (12)
The Bourne Academy, Bournemouth

TRAILS OF THE DEAD

Wandering around in an oversized hospital shirt. Surrounded by trees, a tint of flickering light from an abandoned flashlight. Rustling leaves made the strawberry-blonde teenager jump, whilst her heavy breathing turned into shudders, whispers and cries from those she feared to lose. Fresh and old blood filled the once pure air. She followed the smell which led to even worse. A trail of dead bodies. Jaw chattering, she followed the dead bodies, on and on. She was stopped by a tough grip locked onto her ankle. "He's coming, go!" The strawberry-blonde looked down to see a bloody teenager...

Isabel Mas-Barrett (13)
The Bourne Academy, Bournemouth

YoungWriters
Est. 1991

THE ABANDONED HOUSE

It was dusk. I found myself creeping around in an abandoned house. It was completely dark with only the moonlight pouring in from the smashed windows. A phone rang, I had to answer it. I gradually opened the squeaky door. A cold chill ran through my spine. The room, ominous. Upside-down furniture, smashed windows. I felt so isolated. I edged towards the phone. Fog danced across the floor. My hand shook violently as I picked up the phone. "Hello?" Heavy breathing echoed through the speaker. Something cold pushed down on my shoulders. Wind swirled around the room. Everything went dark...

Megan Fuller (13)
The Bourne Academy, Bournemouth

THE DARKNESS

Swiftly, the fog crawled over the gloomy forest. My eyes taunted me as the moonlight illuminated down onto the decaying house. Suddenly, the gate flung open and a roar of thunder could be heard in the distance. A blood-curdling scream echoed through my head. Leaves crunch as I stepped and the motionless eyes of the house stalked me. Approaching the devilish house my heart started to race. The mossy steps were slippery and squeaky. it's towering over me, the house I haven't seen in eight years. Suddenly, the mist grew heavier, the dark mind-boggling creature appeared in front of me...

Aliz Kadar (13)
The Bourne Academy, Bournemouth

THE ABANDONED HOUSE ON 45TH STREET

The tall, wooden door let out a menacing screech as I entered the abandoned house. My footsteps echoed around the frail walls. Heavy, yet small raindrops hit the green, misty windows with a deafening bang! "Hello?" I whispered, pleading there wouldn't be a response. Rotten floorboards creaked under my shaky feet. I could hear light footsteps above me, scattering along the floor like rats. At least I hoped it was. I turned around slowly, my eyes darting across the corridor. There was an unknown abyss. Then I felt it, a cold, spine-tingling hand crawl across my clammy shoulder...

Daisy-Mae Morgan (12)
The Bourne Academy, Bournemouth

THE CATACOMB

Late at night, Johnny, Daniel, and Sarah enter an abandoned church. They slowly entered through the large doors and saw a massive pattern on the floor. As they started to look around, suddenly the floor shook violently and collapsed.

When they awoke they found themselves in an underground catacomb. Rows upon rows of bodies lined the walls. Suddenly, they stood up and all at once the bodies shouted, "Ruh!" The friends ran as fast as possible, eventually, they found a hole in the wall. As the corpses tried to grab through the hole, the friends realised Daniel was missing...

Aaran Nickless (12)
The Bourne Academy, Bournemouth

THE FOGGY MADNESS

Trees were swaying all around me. I was lost. Branches snapping under my feet. Thick fog was surrounding me like I was trapped in a tornado. And then... *Crack!* "What was that?" I dashed towards the light, hoping I could find someone to help me. "Help, someone, help me! Anyone?" In the distance, I saw a person standing in front of me. Trembling towards them I prayed I would get home. Suddenly, I heard a tremendous scream! "Argh, run!" I turned around and bolted the other way. I tripped. I fell onto something cold. Very cold. Oh, my gracious god...

Chloe Batcock (12)
The Bourne Academy, Bournemouth

LITTLE DID THEY KNOW

It was a house never used. They were running towards it, but little did they know what would happen. The floor creaking as they walked in, dust falling. Taking further steps in, a hunched figure was in the distance. Was the house in use? *Bang!* Could that have been the figure? Following the footsteps of the figure, they peeked through a doorway. There was a piercing chant being muttered, "Leave this house immediately!" the voice chanted repetitively. Gasping, the two children sprinted out of the house with no rest for breaths. But one of them was nowhere to be seen.

Katie Booker (13)
The Bourne Academy, Bournemouth

IS SHE GONE?

The fog was wrapping itself over the trees. I kept walking. "Lily!" I called. I kept on walking in. I had to find her. The moon was peeping over the trees. I stepped. I could hear footsteps around me. "Lily?" I could feel my heart thumping in my chest. "Is that you Lily?" It was dark now, I was scared. "Please Lily." The trees were creaking as I walked under them. I could hear the footsteps coming closer. Suddenly, a hand grabbed my shoulder. Then pain crept up my arm. "Lily... please?" I turned around. I was gone, forever...

Mollie Westerby (12)
The Bourne Academy, Bournemouth

THE DOLL

The doll. It felt like it was staring at me like a bullseye on a dartboard. It had a strange sense about it. I had to get rid of it. I crept towards it. *Slam!* My door slammed shut. "Mum? Mum!" I roared. The last time I checked she was downstairs. Panicking, I grabbed the doll, stormed over to the window, and was about to let go. Suddenly, the doll grabbed me and said, "I'm not going anywhere." Darkness. My eyes slowly opened. Relieved, I said, "It was just a dream."
A hand touched my shoulder, "Yes, just a dream..."

Emily Bartlett (12)
The Bourne Academy, Bournemouth

THE NIGHT BEFORE HALLOWEEN

As I approached the church gates, the smell of dead flowers lingered. The sun was scorching and the flesh of rotten dead bodies opened up a horrid smell. I heard piercing screams but didn't know if I was dreaming. The death chamber was lurking in the distance amongst the mossy trees. The piercing, ear-ringing scream echoed. There I was shaking. The zombies were focused on looking for the blood of their next victim. *Ping!* The bell rang. Twelve o'clock, midnight. The wolves were howling and the church bells rang with all their might to the groan of zombies.

Liam Bashford (12)
The Bourne Academy, Bournemouth

THE ACCIDENT

It was one nice evening and Johnson's family wasn't expecting any tragic events to happen, but out of the blue, there were rocks crashing down on the road, *crash! Bang!* Then Johnson and his family were rumbling down the cliff. The car ripped into many different parts. The eerie silence began. Johnson woke up to find his parent's passed, it was midnight and not one voice could be heard. He spotted a house in the distance, he had no choice but to go. Opening the door hearing a crunch. "Argh!" Then there was a black figure, staring patiently...

Joshua Douglas (12)
The Bourne Academy, Bournemouth

DEOFFREY

Although it was shut, mysterious shadows were lurking, cackles were heard along with deafening screams. All it was, was an abandoned Toys R Us store. The letters were shattered on the terrifyingly blood-infested tarmac. Suddenly, the automatic doors flung open, it was time to have a look inside. "Come and play with these toys," a slow and traumatising voice said. As I edged further, I saw Geoffrey the giraffe with haunting dolls that moved and spoke, "We come to life," one of them said. I was terrified, I couldn't escape all I could see was death!

Charlie Spetch (13)
The Bourne Academy, Bournemouth

YOU CAN'T DO THIS!

"You know you can't do this!" His words became muffled as she shut the creaky door in his face. Her head snapped left like a wind-up toy as a blood-curdling scream was heard. "Hello?" No reply. "Jimmy?" She felt a knot form in her stomach as if she had just seen the most menacing thing ever. Her eyes shut tight as a salty tear formed there; it stung. She cautiously opened them, everything was blurry. Something stood surreal and gothic in front of her. Its slender hands reached for her - breathing heavy, she called for Jimmy. He was gone?

Olivia Tapping (12)
The Bourne Academy, Bournemouth

IN THE WALLS

"Here, it is not that scary," trembled John.

"I dare you to spend a day there," Jack whispered with a grin.

John wandered down the crumbly path to the overgrown garden, the plants towering above as he climbed his way in through a window and mysterious mist covering his only way of escape. The last sign of hope was gone. As he walked further into the house, a clicking noise was heard from upstairs, with each creaky step, the noise seemed to jump from one place to another. The mist crept up the stairs, a heavy breathing coming from within...

Miguel Marques (12)

The Bourne Academy, Bournemouth

THE BLOOD CRUNCHERS

Me, Willow and Noah were on our nightly walk. Down the alleyway by the old abandoned church. *Crunch*, "Hello, who's there?" Willow and Noah were gone. A shiver shot right through me. *Crunch! Bang!* I took a breath. "Hello?" A cold wet hand was on my shoulder. "Don't worry," said a scary dark voice. The shadow of a man appeared in front of me. I felt water, no, blood, running down my face. It covered me like a thick red blanket. I tried to scream then I blacked out and felt someone drag me down to thick gloopy mud...

Evie Clark (12)

The Bourne Academy, Bournemouth

SLAUGHTER HOME

Tuesday 15th March 2017. This was the date Mark Juper was last seen alive. What happened? you ask. Well, this is a summary of the story.

On a rainy school night, Mark walked home passing the abandoned house, he normally saw. That day the house looked peculiar. Smoke came out of the chimney. This hadn't happened in decades. He took his journal that he always wrote in with him so he could write everything he saw.

The floorboards creaked as he walked in. The temperature dropped.

It says in his journal he tried to escape, something was pulling him in.

Mya John-Charles (13)
The Bourne Academy, Bournemouth

UNTITLED

Echoed whispers tiptoed in, following my footsteps as I crept in. I came across an overgrown cottage. "I won't get to the cabin till dawn, I'll ask March to come to pick me up," I mumbled to myself. I called March.

"Look I'll be there as soon as I leave work okay?" she whined.

As I wandered around, ivy climbed the once decorated walls of the master bedrooms, silencing the windows.

Bang! "Hello?" I cried hoping nothing would reply.

"March..?" I questioned as a hand grabbed hand pulled me forward.

Autumn Hall (13)

The Bourne Academy, Bournemouth

AN OLD FRIEND

The lightning flashed right before their eyes. The tall, black house smiled at the two before the gates creaked open slowly. They heard a whisper behind them and they were pushed forward. They carefully crept towards the front door, stepping on small dead flowers. Who brought them here? What did they want? The door flew open. A gust of wind whipped their faces nearly pushing them over. They quietly entered the house. As they entered there was a long corridor with a large set of stairs. A large black figure formed at the top of the stairs. "Hello, Rachel."

Alexis Wilkshire (13)
The Bourne Academy, Bournemouth

THE ADVENTURES OF A HAUNTED HOUSE

A few friends enter a ride at the funfair. They walk in. *This place looks so surreal*, Ruben thinks. Suddenly, a figure jumps out. "Argh, Lauren!" Ruben screams, the others laugh. One suggests they split into two groups of three. "Hey guys, is someone holding my hand? It feels weird. If you can please let go."
What's happening? The others are creeped out and Emily finds a torch and says, "Uhhh, Ruben that's not our hand." They all whisper.
Brooke gives the torch to Ruben... "Argh, I'm leaving."

Ruben Harrison (12)
The Bourne Academy, Bournemouth

THEME SLAUGHTER

"We can't go in!" whispered Frederick.

"Hurry up and follow me you wuss."

As we struggled through the mist, we saw the broken lights from the abandoned theme park. We stopped. The noise of a little girl's laughter was coming from all angles. The gate slammed behind us.

"We should turn back!" exclaimed Frederick.

"Stop being a melon and follow me."

We started sprinting through the maze trying to find the exit. Suddenly, a raspy voice came on the intercom. "You want to play a game?"

Liam Dawson-Deacon (12)

The Bourne Academy, Bournemouth

THE MINE

The fog was stalking me.

"Are you sure about this?" asked Will, with fear swallowing him whole.

"One hundred percent!" I exclaimed with slight doubt in my eyes. Spiders taunted me like the last piece of cake staring you down on your birthday. Cold air brushed my legs like a homeless dog seeking love and warmth. My hands trembled under the lantern. Shadows towered over us, screams erupted from other sections of the cave. *Bang, bang, bang*, the walls were caving in. Blood, sweat and tears for this. All hope is lost for us.

Aiden Blowers (12)
The Bourne Academy, Bournemouth

THE ANGRY GHOST

Rain fell heavily, I needed to find shelter. Suddenly, I spotted an old house and ran towards it. "Hello, is anyone here? Could I shelter from the rain, please?" I asked. Nobody answered. Cautiously, I walked up the creaking steps. As I was entering a room, a chair flew in front of my face. I screamed.

"Why did you enter?" a ghostly voice shouted angrily.

"Who are you?" I squeaked.

"I am a ghost! I will kill you and you will never make it out alive!" the ghost shrieked.

I shivered. Would I get out?

Kira Patel (12)
The Bourne Academy, Bournemouth

HOW DO I ESCAPE?

Running. My heart was racing, I could feel my clammy hands clenching. The thick black fog covered the stale, pungent leaves. They were chasing me. The deathly growls haunted me and their vile mouths clamped onto my skirt. My mind was racing, how would I escape this? How could I defeat them? I faintly saw a house-shaped shadow in the distance. My head pounding, forest trees towering over me. The house shape got clearer and bigger, it called my name. I swung the disintegrating wood-panelled door and shut them out. *Boom!* I prayed I'd stay alive...

Ella Wilson (13)
The Bourne Academy, Bournemouth

DON'T GO IN ALONE

The sun was at its highest point and the birds were singing. The sound of snapping twigs filled the section of abandoned ruins. They were done for. Lizzy and James had been walking in the off-limits zone for an hour but suddenly it went silent, too silent. The wind stopped and it got dark, fog filled the pasture, tension grew as they were separated. They were alone and stranded which was dangerous. Time was slowed and their hearts beat fast. Within a millisecond, there was a large dark paw reaching towards them and the creature let out a chilling scream...

Skye Goldsack (13)
The Bourne Academy, Bournemouth

VALLEY OF SHADOWS

It was here he went missing. Just as the inspector reached the end of the valley he saw nothing but horror. He saw the young missing boy hung on a spear through his chest. The walls had writing on with blood saying: 'You're next'. The inspector called for back-up, but as he was calling for back-up a cold hand gripped onto his mouth. The dark voice said, "Sweet dreams," and the hand gripped on so tightly that the blood gushed out of the inspector's head. His fingers were twitching in pain and the dark voice cackled with mightiness.

George Robson (12)
The Bourne Academy, Bournemouth

MADDY'S STORY

Walking home after meeting her friends, Maddy found herself walking alone down a lit-up road. Feeling someone's presence, she peered behind her to find a middle-aged, bald man stood only metres away with a sinister grin. She quickly scurried away and hid down a dark, desolated alleyway. Fifteen minutes had passed thinking she had lost him, Maddy started to walk down the path. Wanting to make it out alive, she picked up her pace. She reached the end... Something grabbed her from behind, she let out a shriek! But it was too late, she never made it home.

Danielle Illsley (13)
The Bourne Academy, Bournemouth

THE DARK FOREST

As we walked through the dark forest, we found what we were looking for. The old house stood tall but it was still covered in bushes, Millie, Eva, and Ben entered the garden, stinging nettles pulled at their ankles, the door thumped from the inside! "Eva?" called Millie, but she was gone! As Millie and Ben gripped hold of each other they knew they had to get away soon, As fast as they could! Silently, they crept, hoping to not be heard... Until they heard rustling in the bushes, all of a sudden Eva came out, "Boo!!!" Quickly they ran.

Lacy Murphy (13)
The Bourne Academy, Bournemouth

THE CREEPY FOREST

There was mist trapping me in this haunted forest. "Max!" I shouted. "Max, where are you?" I said in a frightened voice. I was approaching a ginormous tree but then heard something, "Callum." I heard in a quiet voice. At first, I thought it was Max but then I was certain it wasn't. But then I heard something. I thought of lots of different feelings. *Will I die? Is it Max? What will happen to me?* Then I felt a tap on my shoulder, "Who's there?" I asked worriedly. But then I was certain who it was...

Edward Isaacs (12)
The Bourne Academy, Bournemouth

GUYS?

Crows surrounded us, me and my friends were searching for a spine-chilling church or house. *Bang.* "Guys?" I exclaimed. I carried on and I went to open the door it was unlocked. The lock must have been busted. Fog swooped in and I couldn't even see my feet then the door creaked open. "Hello?" I went in and there were huge moving shadows. I looked away and shut my eyes, hoping it was a nightmare. They were gone. "Guys, this isn't funny anymore." A chilling hand touched my hand. "Guys?" I squeaked...

Liam Dewet (12)
The Bourne Academy, Bournemouth

THE OMINOUS HALLWAY

As a chilled wind blew down the murky hallway, the little boy stood shivering wailing for his mother. A sudden gust of wind pushed him away from the door. Pushing forward, a life-looking doll sat on a chair shaking its head in a sinister way... he stood mindlessly looking at the door. Feeling uncontrolled, he slowly crept towards the door, attempting to avoid the doll. Blood pouring down the walls, the doll lunged towards, spitting in his face he fell to the ground... The doll loomed over and calmly said with a smirk on its face... "Karma!"

Emily Hall (12)
The Bourne Academy, Bournemouth

THE FIGURE

The wind howled, this was the hour. Silence fell upon the area as I stumbled through the woods, with my feet tripping over twigs. I saw a black silhouette looming in the distance. I idled before approaching the doors of death. The silhouette was watching. But with a blink, it was gone. I trudged on with fear rising inside me. The gates creaked open, beckoning me in. No turning back, my torch flickered on. I scanned the entrance. My heart thumped with every step. A shiver sprinted down my spine. I froze. Footsteps echoed in my ear. I wasn't alone.

Eloise Martin (12)
The Bourne Academy, Bournemouth

THE SCREAM OF GOODBYE

As we climbed over the gate, the doors opened. All was silent but for the tap of rain. I said, "Come on, let's explore the house!"

Katie whispered, "What if someone is here?"

I shrugged my shoulders and sprinted upstairs. As I opened the door it creaked and I laughed. In the corner of my eye I saw something move and said, "Hello?" hoping for a response. I screamed in pain and fell to the ground. Katie panicked and tried to run out the door but it slammed shut. Lightning struck outside and Katie screamed...

Effy Altun (11)
The Bourne Academy, Bournemouth

THE MYSTERIOUS MAN

Walking home late at night with his retired police dog, they got lost in a gloomy, desolate forest. Max, the dog, started to get anxious and began tugging Jakub across the forest, leading him to a menacing, isolated house. The door creaked open. They walked in to see a man stood at the end of the corridor. They decided to approach him for help. They got to the end of the corridor to see that he wasn't there anymore. The door slammed shut and they spun around! The mysterious man reappeared with a bloody machete and started running towards them...

Riley Snell (13)
The Bourne Academy, Bournemouth

THE HOWLER

It was a dark stormy night; the black clouds are concealing the light from the moon. Dave and I are walking home after playing football in the park. A flash of lightning reveals a creepy forest ahead. As we draw closer; we hear the rustling of the leaves on the shaggy trees. I turn to Dave, he's no longer with me. "Dave!" I shouted but my voice is muffled over the howling wind. A stick has crunched behind me, "Dave?" I trembled. I reach for my phone, but there's no signal... and that's when I felt a hand touch me...

Oliver Kieltyka (12)
The Bourne Academy, Bournemouth

INTO THE WOODS

Liz's eyes filled up with fear as her hands started to shake. "Sh-should we go home?" she asked.

"I think we're lost," I said.

We both looked at each other, our fear showing in our faces. The trees surrounded us, trapping us in the darkness. Thunder grew louder as I thought I felt hands on my ankles, but it was probably just the grass. Probably. I turned for a split second but Liz was gone when I looked back. "Liz?" I started to panic. I was alone, alone in the woods. Or that's what I thought...

Jasmin Morris (12)

The Bourne Academy, Bournemouth

THE SPIRIT

Creeeeak, the old brown wooden floorboards were so annoying. I walked towards the stairs even though I didn't get a good feeling in this old isolated house. I didn't want to be a scaredy-cat like Conner. Step by step up the stairs that were creaking loudly as if they were telling me not to go forwards. Obviously, I didn't listen. As I got to the last step, the photos in frames had locked their eyes on me as if I were to do something I would regret. I opened the wooden door. I stepped in. *Stab, thud.* "Oh..."

Laila Ashour (11)
The Bourne Academy, Bournemouth

THE HONKENING BEGINS

Running as quickly as possible I could hear the heavy stomping behind me get louder and louder. The canopy of rotten trees cast shadows all over the leaf-littered ground. I was beginning to get tired, but the fierce adrenaline fought with my muscles to keep me going. Gutteral croaking of ravens ahead stopped as soon as I got closer to the edge of the forest. Sadly, my legs gave up on me and I collapsed. Stomping came to an end. Turning around for a final look, there standing was a terrifying white goose. It approached and my vision went black...

Maria Deka (13)
The Bourne Academy, Bournemouth

THE WITCH IN THE WINDOW

Next to the decrepit old cottage stood a forest darker than night. The long finger-like branches reached for the clouds which opened and let the heavens pour out. I raced for the building, rain like silver bullets on my back. The door almost fell off its hinges. As I escaped the terror, *tap, tap.* The window, a figure, the traditional pointy hat, and a menacing cackle. Cobwebs in my face, my own breath in the derelict rooms. I spun around helplessly, I tried to protect myself but it was too late, the door swung open and I saw it there...

Isla Maher (12)
The Bourne Academy, Bournemouth

A LONG WAY FROM HOME

I was twenty minutes from home when I got a frantic call from my wife. At the start of the call all I heard was heavy breathing sounds, not the kind you get when you just finished a run but the kind you get when you're petrified. "James," she said in a shaky voice, "you need to get here now." This shook me to the core.

"Why?" I said, trying to let her know how scared I was.

"There's someone in the-" The phone cut off and I realised I was going twenty over the limit then out of nowhere...

David Daniels (12)

The Bourne Academy, Bournemouth

UNDEAD CAMP

"James let's go over there!" Ralph said. They came across some tents and blood.

"Ralph we should leave!" James said in a dangerous voice.

"Agreed!" he replied, but they were too late because an army soldier came out of the tent and started to chase them. Then other dead men got off the ground and they smelled like maggots. When they came into the light it looked like they had no skin. They ran until they couldn't and hid in an eerie run-down building and called the police but an army man got them.

Aaron Clark (12)
The Bourne Academy, Bournemouth

THE FORBIDDEN HOUSE

It was a cold, misty day, fog gleamed around my tiny ankles. I could barely see anything, like I was in a dark room with no way out. I kept walking until I bumped into a stiff, damp door. I wanted to open it, so I did. The floor creaked as I slowly walked deeper into the room. My voice echoed as I shouted, "Hello!" I heard something scramble behind me, I quickly turned around, my eyes widened. "There is something here," I mumbled. *Bang!* It came from upstairs. I tiptoed towards the stairs. They shook as I screamed...

Matthew Sholto-Douglas-Vernon (12)
The Bourne Academy, Bournemouth

THE GRAVEYARD

My senses were awakened as we entered the graveyard. I felt isolated, but why? The headstones were crumbling apart. The fog was closing in. It was time to go! I heard a scream. Help! Turning around, I saw the ground shaking, someone was coming up from underground! I walked away. Then all in the space of a minute, someone approached me and touched my shoulder, I looked back and nobody was around. Then they appeared again. There was a hole in the ground, where were they taking me? I was scared! I didn't want to die! Please somebody help me!

Olivia Martin (12)
The Bourne Academy, Bournemouth

RUINED CASTLE

Groaning, Buck struggled to get up from the floor and shook as he got to his feet. Buck wasn't aware why he was unconscious but started to walk around. He was in a ruined castle, the walls were cobbled and collapsing. Suddenly, he heard a crack and peeked around the corner, there was a tall slender figure with glowing eyes which met Buck's, there was silence for three seconds, then there was a deafening screech. Buck darted, tripping in the process, it was chasing him, before it reached him, Buck awoke, on a hospital bed from a coma.

Josh Marshall (13)
The Bourne Academy, Bournemouth

THE MYSTERIOUS CASE OF BILLY BAKER

One normal day, young Billy Baker was home alone, when he heard an unfamiliar sound coming from the basement door. Billy felt a shiver, he slowly shuffled up to the splintering door. He reluctantly grasped the rusty door handle, the door opened with a squeal, a gust of cold damp smelling air hit him in the face. He crept down the mossy staircase, creaking with each step. His legs shaking. The sound stopped, it was darker than the night. Billy was frozen in fear, a cold bony hand grasped his shoulder, the thing let out a menacing cackle...

Ryan Hartwell (13)
The Bourne Academy, Bournemouth

THE HAUNTED HOUSE

There it was, standing still in the darkness. *Smash!* "There goes the window I guess." I crept inside, hoping nothing would attack me. Suddenly, a noise came from the wardrobe. I backed away from the doors. My heart was racing and I began to regret my silly choices as I tiptoed back to the broken window, I could hear noises in the attic. The ladder fell to the floor and two skinny pale legs dangled above before dropping to the floor. My feet were glued to the ground and I didn't have the strength to move or scream...

Ruby Long (12)
The Bourne Academy, Bournemouth

THEME PARK

With just a touch of the rusted lock, the abandoned theme park crashes to the ground. I begin to explore the theme park when a shadow appears out of nowhere. Must be security. Carefully, I crept into the mirror maze. Surely no one will find me. There's some kind of distorted clown music in here, it's creepy. The deeper into the maze, the louder the music gets. This place must have been abandoned for some time. It smells like something rotten and... blood. I feel hot breath on my neck and look to see a clown holding a knife. Argh!

Phoebe Palmer (12)

The Bourne Academy, Bournemouth

WHAT WAS IT?

Footprints surrounded me! Thunder rumbled. I wasn't alone! I ran like a cheetah searching for its prey, my breathing was loud, it followed me.

The trees towered over me as I saw it. Glass everywhere. I crept around it as I came to the door. Bang! "Hello?" There was no reply.

Slowly, I took a step at a time and locked the door behind me. I thought I saw something in the shadows following my every step.

I hide behind the closest thing I could find, maybe a chair? I moved myself to a worn-out closet. I was found...

Lexie Cliffe (13)
The Bourne Academy, Bournemouth

THE FIGURE

It was foggy. I couldn't see a thing as leaves swooped around me. It was cold.
Slowly creeping forward into the darkness I felt somebody walking behind me, but nobody was there. An icy breath blew onto my ear. A finger ran across my spine. I froze. Looking around, nothing. I ran. All of a sudden, my body stopped. Something was dripping on me, it wasn't rain... It was red. My breath got faster, my legs turned to jelly. My heart was trying to jump out of me. I turned and saw a tall figure.
"You're next..."

Holly Carley-Lamb (12)
The Bourne Academy, Bournemouth

ALONE IN A FOREST

As I traversed through the shadowy forest, I felt a chilling breeze brush across my face, all of a sudden I heard a sound, it murmured across the forest and my heart began to pulse. The snapping sound of a branch crunched behind my back, something was here, I was not alone. I took a deep breath and turned around. My eyes scanned the forest, nothing. I continued walking knowing I was being watched. *Crunch, crunch.* "What was that?" I had to get out of this place fast. Then, a cold bony hand touched my right shoulder...

Jaydn Hardy (12)
The Bourne Academy, Bournemouth

THE ABANDONED BARN

I had no clue where I was, I was in the middle of a field. I carried on walking forward hoping I would find something. After ten minutes I found a barn, it looked old and abandoned. I got closer. *This might be a good place to stop and rest.* The windows were smashed, glass on the floor. I slowly creaked the door open and peered inside. I shouted, "Hello!" There was no reply so I walked in. I took a walk around, I accidentally kicked a trough and jumped. Near the back, I heard a loud thud. "Who's there?"

Chelsea Johnston (12)
The Bourne Academy, Bournemouth

THE HORRIBLE EXPERIENCE

Hauntingly, an owl came to a spooky abandoned graveyard. A little later, I heard a massive loud bang. "What was that?" I said. "Let's go and find out where it's coming from!" When we started to walk to find where the bang came from, we started to hear some loud footsteps coming from the creepy cold forest. So we split up to have a look at who the footsteps come from. After a few moments, I heard a loud scream, so I dashed for my life and I found my friend. He was dead. So we stayed with him until...

Jayden Rodger (12)
The Bourne Academy, Bournemouth

THE HAUNTED HOUSE

As the sun went down, I walked past an abandoned house that stood there crumbling. Slowly, I crept towards the house and went in. As I opened the cold, damp door, a shiver went down my spine. I could hear my friends saying, "No, don't go in there!" An infestation of rats screeched and scrambled out the door. As I opened it I could hear the bitter wind scratching against the walls of the so-called haunted house. I felt a strange brush against my arm that passed me as the wind stopped. Was it the wind or something else?

Tia-Louise Tuck (2)
The Bourne Academy, Bournemouth

RUNNING FROM MONSTERS

Frantically sprinting through the house, I gasped for air. Almost at the entrance, I couldn't wait for the bitter wind to bite my face again. I gave myself a moment to breathe. Hearing footsteps, I knew I had to run! The ball of dread built inside in my throat. I ran! Metres from the entrance, I spat out the cobwebs in my mouth. *Creeeaak!* The door coincidently opened. Sighing in relief, I leaped out of the building. The thick, heavy rain rapidly hit my face. Finally, I was safe from the monster lying within, or was I?

Michael Farrow (13)
The Bourne Academy, Bournemouth

ALONE IN THE VILLAGE

Dead crows were hanging on the tree, while I was walking through the dark, groggy forest. There was grunting in the background as I ran towards the village. Time passed swiftly and the grunting came closer and the fog filled the sky. There was no hope for me to find any humans in this old, abandoned village. I looked and looked for someone to help me get out of this place. Slowly, I crawled into a house in the village while searching for any weapons to defend me from the grunting noise. Crawling out, I noticed the creepy castle...

Teyla Cave (12)
The Bourne Academy, Bournemouth

THE HOUR OF MYSTERY

The fog was rolling in. I found an old abandoned house. There was music playing. Old, creepy music. The creepy house got the better of me. As did the curiosity that was building inside of me. I went in, "Hello?" No answer. *Bang!* I found a ghostly figure. Suddenly, I heard a deathly screech. Thick fog tumbled from the stairs. "No!" I heard someone bellow. "Not Sophie!" The voice bellowed again. Then an old bony hand yanked me down. The very last noise I made was a screech from the pit of hell.

Sophie Hill (12)
The Bourne Academy, Bournemouth

THE SUNSET

I looked up and saw Archie. He'd been my best friend since I moved. I grazed my hand on a fallen rough tree and looked up to see the sun's gaze fading. "That's bad," Archie said. Suddenly, "Run, we have to go!" he screamed before I could even blink he took my hand and darted like a cheetah away, yanking me alongside him. I was so confused he'd never done this before. Then suddenly I heard a hideous scream echoing from behind the trees. I started to feel my heartbeat faster and faster with fear.

K Green (13)

The Bourne Academy, Bournemouth

WOLF BLOOD

It was midnight as the clouds gathered, birds were singing and the wind howled. There was an abandoned house. I walked nearer and nearer, my heart was pounding like the beat of a drum. I opened the door, "Hello, is anyone there?" The living room door opened. I jumped back, something or someone was there! I thought, *no, it cant be.* It was coming towards me, I flung the door open and ran as fast as I could. I heard the paws of a great giant bear. I looked behind me, it disappeared. I panicked and ran home safely.

Liberty Bond (13)
The Bourne Academy, Bournemouth

HER HOUSE

A shiver crawled down my spine. The thick fog, wiping out everything around it. I crept up to the house, spiders crawling down the wooden planks. The door was open ajar. I went in. Every footstep made a noise. *Creak, creak, creak.* I shuffled upstairs a cold breeze slapped my face. One by one, I tilted my head into each room. Nothing. It was all in my head. I let out a heavy sigh of relief. As I headed downstairs, I was stopped in my tracks. There. She was there. Stood, blocking the door. Dirty dress, black hair. Silence.

Ella-Grace Tyrrell (13)

The Bourne Academy, Bournemouth

THE MAN

Snow cascaded towards the ground. My fingers felt like they were about to fall off. I couldn't hear a thing. Suddenly, I felt a sense of unease. Like someone was watching me. Beginning to walk quicker, I got more worried. All of a sudden, a wrinkly hand touched me on the shoulder. I pushed it off and sprinted into the crooked old house. There was blood all over the door. When I opened the door, it ripped off. Crime scene signs were everywhere. I ignored them. The man was right on my tail. I rushed up the stairs. I turned...

Jensen Fox (12)
The Bourne Academy, Bournemouth

FRIDAY THE 13TH PART XI - THE HOUSE

He walks through the desolate, foggy, empty forest with his friend Yon. They both tread through the dark, misty forest. They peer behind them, they see a tall, muscular man with a hockey mask and a bloody machete in his hand. They both run into a house, as soon as they entered the frozen air hits them both in the face. They run in and slam the door shut. Yon stands in front of the door when... The machete goes through the door and through Yon's stomach... They both fall, one in death and one in fear. There's no escape.

Kain Dix (13)
The Bourne Academy, Bournemouth

THE DEATH THREATS

This town is falling apart. Ten bodies were completely drained of blood. The town was frantic since the last attacks. Nobody was safe. The victims of the attacks were from the founding families. If you're reading this, mine might be next.

The next day, another murder happened. My mum. I was the first person to find her body hanging in the kitchen.

I was at my friend's house, there was a bad and weird smell in there like a dead corpse. I thought it was the killer, if you read this I'm probably the next...

Chloe Calvert (11)
The Bourne Academy, Bournemouth

ONE DAY...

In the distance, my eyes were filled with fear as I saw the abandoned house. Ivy and cobwebs shielded the house as sunlight wouldn't be able to penetrate the water-stained windows. I marched onto the doorstep, the door squeaked open. Placing my foot onto the floorboard. I took a deep breath of the melancholy air as dust brushed along my skin. Old family photos were hung above a leather sofa that hadn't felt cosy in a long time. Suddenly, the wind howled, the door slammed shut. I tried to pull it open, would I get out?

Lujin Houari (12)
The Bourne Academy, Bournemouth

DEATH STORM

Just as I was about to enter the graveyard, a storm rolled in. *Should I go back?* I thought to myself. "No," I said. "No, no, no." I went over to my friend's grave but something was wrong with it. The headstone had been moved. A strike of lightning struck the ground and scared me. Then the ground moved and the headstone moved. I fainted. A few hours later I woke in a random house. I was chained up to a chair with tape over my mouth. *Creeaak.* A door opened. Bang. A gunshot went off...

Alex Sherring (12)
The Bourne Academy, Bournemouth

BONES

Clouds grew grey over my head as I crept down the concrete steps. Moss coated the steps in clumps. It was isolated and all there was was an eerie silence. In front of me was a wooden door that creaked at each gust of wind. I stepped inside and a putrid smell filled my nose. I thought hard about it. Bodies. Dead bodies. I stepped forward, *crunch*. Was it a snail? I look down into the pitch-black. I plunged forward, grabbing what was under my foot. I dropped it, letting out a gasp. Bone. I tried running for the door.

Sophie Mandley (12)
The Bourne Academy, Bournemouth

WEDDING DAY

As I hurried home from the thunder, I heard wedding bells in the distance, I thought, *shelter.* I hurried into the church and all was silent. No one was there. Or so I thought. All was pitch-black. As I turned to leave, the church doors locked. I was stuck in the church. Suddenly, laughter filled the room and the music was back. I was dancing by myself. My body wasn't in control. Neither was my mind. I was possessed. Suddenly, my body was on the floor, blood surrounded me. Turned out I was the bride all along.

Lorelei Houson (13)

The Bourne Academy, Bournemouth

THEIR HOUSE

We recently moved into an old mansion. My sister tells me scary stories every night since we moved, about dead children and monsters under the bed. Of course, I don't believe it but it still gives me the shivers. The second week of us living here, I heard an unusual noise, I went downstairs to see what it was and it was coming from the walls. I opened the walls and saw something I really regret seeing, I saw around fifteen dead children in the walls. I ran away but something was following me, it was my dead brother...

Lily Hillier (12)
The Bourne Academy, Bournemouth

THE BLOOD-CURDLING CHURCH

It was a misty night, far from home. I saw a church. I didn't think about ghosts or demons, just warmth. I ran inside. The cobwebs glistened in the moonlight as the door thudded behind me. I tiptoed around the church as screams filled my head, I sat down on the cold stone floor. Suddenly, something tapped my shoulder, I rose up like my spirit was dragging me outside. I zoomed up above the church spire, all of a sudden I fell. My life flashed before my eyes as the cold metal pierced my skin. The whole world went black.

Amelia Catmull (12)
The Bourne Academy, Bournemouth

THE LEGEND OF THE VAMPIRES

Faster than lightning, rapid healing, unbelievable strength. This creature can do things that are supposed to be impossible. I sat, heart thudding waiting in silence. What was it? Why was it here? What was it going to do to me? Bravely, I stepped out of my car to face this creature. It was immortal. Creature of the night. I stuttered as I said the word, "Vampire?" I ran as fast I could but he was too fast, my eyes began to open. I felt this thirst go through me except it wasn't water I craved, it was blood!

Imogen Roach (12)

The Bourne Academy, Bournemouth

ALIEN ISOLATION

Waiting, waiting, waiting... Tiptoeing around the room quietly as a mouse. Then a sudden shriek of what seemed to be a humanoid creature. I crept closer. The sudden urge of reality hit me. It was clear I was not alone in this house. This thing was on the hunt, hunting for me. This was now a fight for survival, the rain hammered on the windows, the thunder rumbled. As I turned the corner I saw it... The seven-foot-tall thing. Three spiked, four arms, two legs. Now I was certain I was not alone. It stood watching, waiting.

Logan McDonnell (13)
The Bourne Academy, Bournemouth

MYSTERIOUS CREATURE

There I was, standing far away from the dark, damp house. Curiously, I took slow small steps. I could hear cars rushing and branches snapping behind me! I thought it was a cat, but something got closer and closer each time I looked at it. My heart was pounding. I ran towards the house to hide. Wondering who or what it was. I sat in the corner and waited until I could not hear anything except my deep breathing. I heard footsteps coming from every direction. I thought I was going crazy until I heard a door creak open...

Alisha Culwick (12)
The Bourne Academy, Bournemouth

A DREAM OR NOT?

You creep closer towards your spot to read, a breeze of fog rushes towards you like a happy puppy... You plop yourself down and pull out a book. Unexpectedly, you fall down a creepy, cob-webby hole. You feel spiders all over you. You get to the end and see an old house. Then stumble up to the door but before you can knock, you hear rustling inside and force your way in. All you can smell is panic in the mossy air, blood rushing down your cheek, you see a tall figure, it gets closer, then you can't see anything...

Aysha Roberts (13)
The Bourne Academy, Bournemouth

THE MISSING GIRL

It was almost night, the cold breeze was blowing my face. An abandoned house was across the road, It was a gloomy, cold night. I had no other choice but to go in. Assuming nobody was there, I crept in. Shivering, the door opened slowly, "Hello?" I mumbled. The door slammed behind me, sweat drooled down my back. I tiptoed up the stairs. "Is anyone here?" I whispered. A door swung open slowly. My heart pounding. *Bang!* "Who's there?" I yelled. A cold hand touched my shoulder...

Emily Li (11)
The Bourne Academy, Bournemouth

POISON IVY

It was beautiful. It was a gorgeous silk dress but it missed something, shoes. Elegantly I put my feet in. Much better. I looked like Poison Ivy with my ginger hair and my green dress. Then I saw it. A cloaked figure put its long bony fingers onto my shivering shoulder. *Bam!* the light began to fade. My anxiety took over me. And I froze. It cackled. Looking down, I saw ivy crawling up my leg. It slithered up like a snake. It grew rapidly and strangled me until I had no soul left in me. It left me, lifeless.

Veda Maqsudi (12)
The Bourne Academy, Bournemouth

THE GIRL ON THE SWING

Slowly, my senses awakened. I saw that I'd come to a creepy isolated graveyard. Surrounded by dead rotten people, I stood up and saw one of the graves. It said: 'If you dare to enter you won't be stopped, watch your back before the timer stops'. As I was about to turn back, I heard a creepy baby laugh. I could see a little girl crying on a swing, blood on her white dress, she was singing 'ring around the roses'. "I want to kill you." I started running and tripped over something...

Brooke Dunning (12)
The Bourne Academy, Bournemouth

MY BEST FRIEND'S GRAVEYARD

There was a graveyard just in the distance. Kelly started to walk towards it. "Stop!" I yelled. Kelly started to run. I ran after her. She stopped when she got to the entrance, there were trees surrounding us and there was a smell I had never smelt before, it was disgusting. Then she turned, her eyes were pure black, there was a deadly scream. She walked into the graveyard. I followed slowly and quietly. Then she sat next to a stone and I started to hear a cry, what I saw next made me run away screaming.

Natasha Daniels (12)
The Bourne Academy, Bournemouth

WHAT WAS THAT?

I creaked the door open and walked in as slowly as possible, the room was pitch-black with only a dim, blinking flashlight as a light source. The floor was covered in crusty boxes. I turned to the damp wall behind me and attempted to turn on the light switch. *Click!* A shock jolted up my arm but nothing. *Click.* I automatically turned the switch off as if it had turned on. Shaking my hand up and down, I turned around and headed over to the flashlight. Carefully I picked it up, a flash of colour...

Enya Weir (12)
The Bourne Academy, Bournemouth

THE NIGHT IT ALL WENT WRONG

I need to listen more. I can't believe I've been so stupid after all Mum said, I didn't listen. But here I am, lost all by myself at night! All I knew was that I had to find shelter and fast! Suddenly thousands of crows attacked me. Trying to find my way, I stumbled into a church. I knew I shouldn't go in but I was cold and it was dark. I ran in! This was far from a normal church. It was abandoned! There were bones scattered up the aisle. There were so many noises, my head was spinning...

Sky Stratton (12)
The Bourne Academy, Bournemouth

THE GATE

During a midnight stroll, I bumped into a gate. It belonged to an abandoned house. I lay my hand on it, everything went black. I woke up in the house, watched the sunrise, then tried to escape. It was locked. I decided to explore. I saw an axe nearby, went up the creaky stairs then saw a skeleton. Took no notice then turned away and explored. I went back. it wasn't there. I ran for the axe and grabbed it. I felt a cold finger touch my back. Nothing was there. I turned back, it was there... holding the axe...

Jasmine Wright (12)
The Bourne Academy, Bournemouth

THE GRAVEYARD

I went into a forest. It was dark and gloomy, the trees were shaking. I heard footsteps all around me. I kept walking. In the middle of the forest, there was an abandoned house. There was fog all around the house, I tripped over a tree stump. I opened the door of the house, there was loud squeaky noise. I got scared, I went out the back door, there was a grave, someone was banging the grave. I found someone's head popping out from the grave. I ran fast as I could, people were coming out from nowhere...

Inayat Begum-Singleton (12)
The Bourne Academy, Bournemouth

THE BASEMENT

I've been hearing voices ever since Grandma died, her last words were, "Look in the basement." It was a good idea in the daylight. The door screeched like it was in pain. I grabbed a bat and put it behind my back just in case. I saw an old photo of me in the other room, it was me on my second birthday, Grandma always gave me the best memories. But then I saw blood crawling from a different room, it was the same man who visited Grandma the day before she died, but then I saw my dead parents...

Maisie-Mae Irvine (12)
The Bourne Academy, Bournemouth

THE TWIST

Floorboards creaking, wind howling and the moon shining, we were all on the porch. I opened the door and instantly got some dusty cobwebs in my face and then the door slammed shut. Suddenly, opera music played upstairs. I didn't see my friends so I went upstairs, each stair screaming with a creak. I got to the top but then I got jump-scared by a rat and I ran to the room only to see a floating crib! I realised this was the end of me but then all my friends jumped out and said, You got pranked!"

Lukas Bailey (13)
The Bourne Academy, Bournemouth

THE TRAIN ACCIDENT

Today was the day, it was the last time he would cross the abandoned tracks. He was moving the next week and had to pack. As he was crossing he heard a child's voice. He went to investigate and found a small girl lying unconscious on the tracks, he picked the small child up and went to his apartment. He went to bed, the next morning, he went downstairs, but the child was gone. Instead, there was a newspaper about a train crash that happened years ago on this day. He saw the girl dead in the picture.

Iliana Bevan (12)
The Bourne Academy, Bournemouth

THE CHURCH

As the stars were making their way out, I knew that I wouldn't be able to make it home on time. I saw a church, it looked old and filthy but I made my way over there. I called out for Olivia but I couldn't hear an answer. I walked up to the door, it opened! There were long, thin corridors and as I got almost to the end I heard a noise. Footsteps! They were coming closer to me. I covered my eyes in fear! A hand touched my shoulder. As I turned around there was nobody there, "Olivia?"

Elizabeth Liberty (12)
The Bourne Academy, Bournemouth

THE FORBIDDEN FOREST

One day on an adventure, I spotted a bright vibrant forest filled with soothing blue rivers and sunshine beaming down on it. But at dusk the forest began illuminating and it looked like a storm was on the horizon. Then suddenly there was a scream and it started to thunder, it didn't feel comforting anymore. As I crept closer and closer, *boom!* Thunder struck in front of me as if it were a warning...
I found a gate, as I was unlocking it a cold, shrivelled hand touched my shoulder...

Alex Harris (12)
The Bourne Academy, Bournemouth

THE FRIGHTENING FEARS

I stumbled into the gloomy, horrid forest. Slowly my senses awoke, I could hear everything. The menacing murder of crows above the possessed trees. Bugs crawled up my leg, shivering as they moved. I regretted everything. I unfroze and continued walking, with every crunch of the leaves and the petrifying fog, I slowly found myself getting deeper and deeper into the forest. Standing there were towering shadows, stood around me, my heart paced as footsteps surrounded me. I knew there was no going back.

Mia Dillon (12)
The Bourne Academy, Bournemouth

THE PHONE

As I walk through the forest, leaves bustle across my face, then all the trees stop, creating a weird format, a circle, the smell of wood fighting the air. In the middle, there it lies, a manor. My curiosity gets the best of me so I go inside, each step making me more scared, like a cup full of fear about to overflow, every creak, every step. But then I hear it, a phone. My body starts to freeze. I run out of there with the imaginary cup overflowed. I decide to walk back in and it's behind me...

Ethan Searley (12)
The Bourne Academy, Bournemouth

THE LIGHT EYES

I stumbled through the woods whilst the fog was creeping in, it was getting dark, *I should call Jack*. I thought. I saw an old church. I went inside and I heard books getting knocked over. I rushed downstairs and I saw a deep and dark long hallway. I turned around and I saw light eyes down the hallway, I walked up to them and while I was going down the hallway, it kept getting colder. Then I turned around for a second I felt two hands on my shoulders. "Jack? Is that you?" I said...

Marc Dediu (12)
The Bourne Academy, Bournemouth

CHURCH

Next to me was a church, I ran to the door when I heard footsteps behind me, the handle fell off when it waved open staring at me. My senses woke up when it creaked open. My hair stood up, the floor vibrated and I hit my head on a painting. Suddenly, it stopped. I felt tingles running in-between the bones of my spine. I walked over to the seats. I heard a bang then a scream coming from the graves. I crept outside and crawled around them. I heard more footsteps, someone had grabbed me from behind...

Daniel Gilbert (12)
The Bourne Academy, Bournemouth

I SHOULD HAVE GONE HOME

It was almost dark, there was no way I was getting home now. There were lights flying everywhere blocking my view. Suddenly, I saw an old house, there was nowhere else, I had to go in. I ran inside, slamming the door behind me, making the whole house shudder. The first thing I saw was a huge rusty staircase. I stepped on one of the stairs, sneezing from the dust. I was going to stay here till the storm stopped. Suddenly I felt a cold hand on my shoulder. Help me!
I should have just gone home!

Stephanie Howard (12)
The Bourne Academy, Bournemouth

BENEATH THE SHADOWS

It was another dark evening. After all my friends had left. I was walking home. I was so tired and wanted to take a break from walking. I could see a house in the distance, it only took me five minutes to walk there. It was dull. I quietly opened the door, desperately hoping that there would be some sort of seat for me to rest on. I took a small step in and immediately reached for my flashlight, the old floorboards creaked and it made me jump. My light flickered, I knew this was a very bad idea...

Isobel Golding (12)
The Bourne Academy, Bournemouth

THE TREE WHITE SILENCE

I stumbled through the woods. The bushes rustled and I immediately jumped. I thought it was just a dog so I walked on. The fog was blinding. The fog made the branches look like arms, they looked like they could reach out and grab me. I felt a chill run down my spine. I walked into a tree, but it wasn't there before. I turned around and to my horror, there was a slimy white figure staring down at me. It grabbed me by the collar and dragged me. I let out a shrill scream. That was it. Game over.

Daniel Drury-Wright (12)
The Bourne Academy, Bournemouth

THE ABANDONED HOUSE

I trudged along the gravel road, the fog crept around the musky trees. All of a sudden, I could hear deafening music and blood-curdling singing. I could see an abandoned house up ahead. I tiptoed up to the door, but it was locked. I could see something shiny below my feet, a key! I tried the key on the lock. It worked! As I plodded in, the singing turned into a little girl humming. My brain sent shivers down my whole body. I felt as if it was going to melt. I felt a cold hand hold my shoulder...

Emily Soady (12)
The Bourne Academy, Bournemouth

ABANDONED

I woke up, slowly I looked to find myself next to an abandoned mansion with Harrison next to me. The mansion took up my whole peripheral vision. I looked around, we were in a forest. I could hear the voices whispering, they were probably the past people who died before. We entered the house, it was pitch-black, the floor creaked underneath us. Not knowing what was in front of us, suddenly, the door shut loudly. I looked back to find Harrison screaming and getting taken away into the darkness...

Oliver Pollitt (13)
The Bourne Academy, Bournemouth

THE HAUNTED HOUSE

I walked through the leaves to see the haunted house stood ahead of me, calling my name. The cobwebs filled the room, the musty smell on the tip of my tongue. I automatically jumped out of my skin as I turned around. I saw a mannequin glaring at me. I crept upstairs and walked down the dark corridor. The silence filled my ears. I turned my head and heard a high-pitched scream. I sprinted out onto the garden, as I left I turned around, it was there, the mannequin, staring right into my eyes...

Ella Somers (12)
The Bourne Academy, Bournemouth

THE MAN IN THE MIST

Bang! The door swung open and a crazy man appeared. Ben screamed and ran to the other side of the church, the man slowly came towards him but this time there were more of them. Ben was hiding in a corner, he got his phone out but it was dead. He tried to move but the floorboards creaked too loudly. Ben got up and could hear the wind whistle through the window and it had just started to rain. Ben didn't know what to do but then felt a wet hand on his shoulder, his heart stopped...

Oliver Bartlett (12)
The Bourne Academy, Bournemouth

THE VAMPIRE ATTACK

"Argh!" An ear-piercing scream was heard for miles away as the girl stood frozen, staring at the lifeless body. Another scream. It was a heart. Still beating but only just. It had been ripped out. It was another vampire attack. She started running for her life and with every step, dead bodies drained of blood fell at her feet. Panting became faster when the end got close."Don't move, don't scream," was whispered ever so quietly. Was she going to make it out alive?

Sophie-Mae Chick (12)
The Bourne Academy, Bournemouth

THE MIRROR

I looked around my new room. It only had a bed, a drawer, and a huge mirror. In the drawer there was a note 'Cover the mirror, don't let it take you'. "Probably a prank," I said to myself.

That night, I slept without a blanket, it was dark and cold but I didn't dare find out if the note was true. I woke up and could hear a faint whisper, "Help, help, I'm trapped, help me out!" I reached my hand into the mirror, a portal?

"Gotcha!"

Ella Bullen (13)
The Bourne Academy, Bournemouth

THE ABANDONED CIRCUS

In 1869 on a gloomy, foggy night, a man named Jerry was travelling through the forest when he saw a red and white striped tent. As he crept towards it he saw that it was an abandoned circus tent in the middle of the forest. It started to rain so he sought shelter in the tent. As he entered he saw hundreds of chairs filled with one-eyed dolls. But as he got to the centre of the tent all the dolls stood up and ran at Jerry. He looked up and a skeleton clown jumped on him, he screamed...

Jack Smith (12)

The Bourne Academy, Bournemouth

THE DARK, GLOOMY CHURCH

When I entered that creaky church I knew I was in danger! As soon as I got inside I could see that the church was overgrown. I walked forward and I saw a trapdoor. I snuck into the basement and heard a bang! I kept walking. As I was walking I could feel the cold breeze knowing that this church was really, really old. I wanted to go back but I knew I was brave! I felt another breeze like someone was behind me. I took one more step then looked back. There was a Slenderman. I was dead...

Callum Casserley-Pyne (12)
The Bourne Academy, Bournemouth

THE THREE BOYS

Once upon a time, three boys named James, Blade and Jim were safe at home but they decided to go to the forest very late at night. As they got to the forest Blade felt like they were being watched so he looked around and saw a tall red-eyed figure smiling so they ran as far as they could and ended up running into an abandoned church. James got a stone and used it to get into the church. After they got in they fell asleep except Blade, he decided to wander around but was never found.

Cameron Dillon (12)
The Bourne Academy, Bournemouth

FRIDAY 13TH

I was sitting on my bed like I usually do on a Friday night, but this Friday was different, this Friday was special because it was Friday the thirteenth at precisely twelve o'clock. It was dark, it was creepy, it was scary. I got up from my bed to go get my favourite toy from the basement, why it was in there I had no clue? But this time it was in a box, I was wondering why, it wasn't the last time. So why now? I went to go back to bed.

"Hello," said a voice.

Courtney Arnold (12)
The Bourne Academy, Bournemouth

THE CLOWN

I was at the normal circus with my mum and dad. I was there for so long and then people started leaving. We were the only people there, well one other person, a clown! It was standing still, I blinked and I disappeared, then I heard my mum scream. I turned around and my mum's body was there dragged along the floor. I heard lots of clown noises, I turned and he was standing there and I screamed. Then he jumped at me, it all went black and I realised it was over, I had died.

Lewis Philogene-Jones (12)
The Bourne Academy, Bournemouth

THE HOUSE

The haunting, horrifying, horrid house hid behind the trees in the dark black sky all that could be seen was one window and the worst thing was that there was someone in the house. But it hadn't been looked at for over ten years. This boy named Tom went for a walk and saw the house so went in and nobody ever saw him again. Then one day the girl named Hannah also went for a walk and also saw the house and checked it and then she screamed, that was it, nobody will see her.

Shorinne Davis (12)
The Bourne Academy, Bournemouth

HELP!

As I entered, I saw a lot of stairs. When I stepped on one it creaked so loud that I got scared. When I finally came to the top I saw a shadow and I looked again and they were gone. I got my torch and walked, I saw paintings but I felt like somebody was watching me. I looked back and saw the same shadow, I was terrified. I then saw a person, I ran so fast. I saw blood and heard scraping. Then I ran out of the house and somebody followed me, then I screamed: "Help!"

Letisha Lillington (12)
The Bourne Academy, Bournemouth

THE ALLEYWAY

I was walking home from my friend's house to mine. I went down a gloomy alleyway where it gave me bad vibes. So I went down the gloomy alleyway and I heard a scream so I backed up and something touched my shoulder. Slowly as a tortoise, I turned my head and saw the most terrifying non-skin person wearing a black cloak and holding a scythe. I pelted it to my house then I tripped over my two feet and suffered some painful damage to my legs. Then it was in front of me...

Jamie Dean (12)
The Bourne Academy, Bournemouth

THE CRASH

James crashed. He crawled out of the car in pain. His parents were dead, in the distance he saw a crooked, wooden house. Even though the pain was killing, he made his way up to the house. Before he touched the door, it swung open. In front of him were the rotten stairs. Slowly, he went up the stairs holding his stomach in pain. A door slammed in his face. He slowly opened the door. A glowing light came out of the closet. He opened the door and was never seen ever again.

Fynnley Youngs (12)
The Bourne Academy, Bournemouth

THE NUN

I was on holiday, while I was on holiday I went to the church. When I was there it was dark, empty, and cold. It looked abandoned and haunting, but I still went in. I saw lots of red liquid, it was blood. There were dead nuns, except for one bloody one, she was standing and being still like a statue. As I stepped once, the nun twisted her neck and smiled at me then chased me. I was running for my life. She was catching up to me, then I tripped...

Jake Gostling (12)
The Bourne Academy, Bournemouth

THE DEMON IN THE BASEMENT

As I wander the forest, a flickering light catches my eye. I follow the light to find a silent mansion stood alone in the forest. I crept into the cold, open hallway, and the door slams shut behind me. Outside, wolves are howling and scratching at the door. I'm trapped. I head up the unstable stairs and then feel my body being dragged back down. My fear could be smelled from miles away when I suddenly notice a black figure, I'm shaking...

Maya Punal (12)

The Bourne Academy, Bournemouth

THE DARK FOREST

The mist came storming into my face as I walked cautiously into the shadowy forest. I had to pray for my life as I was far from home so whatever happens, happens. As I approached the middle of the forest, I could see all the bats that had lived there. Soon after, they had flown away from me. I saw many different shadowy hallucinations and found myself hanging onto one of the swaying trees for dear life, then, all I saw was pitch-black.

Dania Hamadi (11)
The Bourne Academy, Bournemouth

THE LAST NIGHT

The cold rainy night fell upon us, I unlocked the ancient steel door and I entered. I saw nothing but darkness, the freezing raindrops dripped down the back of my spine, sending a nasty chill to my whole body. I tiptoed up the crackling, creaking stairs and then I got to the top. On the wooden, fragile door was a note saying: 'Run', suddenly I felt a delicate hand on my shoulder, I slowly turned around...

Alfie Messom (13)
The Bourne Academy, Bournemouth

CRIES OF THE SOLDIER

I thought going to sleep in my own bed would make a change. But no. The sound of the tanks fills my head. I can taste the sweat dripping down my cold, damp face. I can hear the cries of fallen soldiers shouting for help. My friend Sam died in my cold arms in the war. I can hear his scream to this day. I then feel something touch my back, I turn around, nothing is there. Then there it is... Argh!

Max Perkins (13)
The Bourne Academy, Bournemouth

THE MAN

Whistling through the cracked glass ceiling, the wind cast a faint breeze. Paper scattered across the concrete ground, soaked in a strange goo. A sinister sight. A cold shiver burst down my spine, making me regret ever coming here. My head spun, everything became a blur. I was stopped, a hand rested on my shoulder. A pale man stood in front of me, eyes black and he was covered in blood...

Logan Reddick (13)
The Bourne Academy, Bournemouth

THE CANNIBAL

They were walking alone, silent. Leon whispered, "I'm going to go ahead." I knew he was desperate so I let him go ahead. Time went on, I couldn't find him. I went further into the forest, the light faded the further in I went. I froze at the foul sight. Chunks of Leon were everywhere. I heard a cackle from behind. I turned but no one was there...

Alexander Wakefield (13)
The Bourne Academy, Bournemouth

THE HOUSE

"Stop!" I shouted, using up all my breath! But it was too late, my friend had already entered the isolated, abandoned house. Frantically, I started chasing after him because I knew something wasn't right. But, as I made it to the door, I heard a scream. I edged in, I saw that the basement door was open and someone was looking up at me...

Jake Carr (13)
The Bourne Academy, Bournemouth

THE SLAUGHTER HOUSE

We started running, our hearts were pounding in our ears. We saw it. That explained why it was called 'The Slaughter House'. We were just going to pray. It was like someone was in the room. And odd presence. We were all still together, not for long though. I was sweating. My palms were sweating. We were always on our guard, waiting for someone, something to jump out. One by one we were taken. We didn't know where though. It suddenly went eerily quiet. The moon casts its freakish shadows on the blood-red floor. Would I be next?

Harvey Whitehead (12)
Venn Boulevard Centre, Kingston Upon Hull

THE HOUSE

Creak, we entered the house. All we could see in the darkness was furniture covered in white sheets and cobwebs. I was exploring the house while my friends went looking around. But I heard a bang, I turned around and the sofa had gone. I was scared, my body was shaking and before I could do anything I heard another bang. It came from the kitchen and I could hear my friends screaming, then I turned around, something pulled me and I got dragged into a basement. I found all my friends, they all looked dead. Was I next?

Layla Kirk (12)
Venn Boulevard Centre, Kingston Upon Hull

EYES OF MADNESS

"Hurry up Lila, we might lose them!" April shouted.

In the thickness of the forest, a voice shouted back, "Sorry but I hate running!"

"Is it just me or is it starting to go dark?" asked Lila.

"Yes, why?"

"It isn't supposed to be for hours!" questioned Josh.

"Argh!" shrieked Lila as the last of the light was gone.

There was a rush of wind making April's hair swish in her face. The school trip wasn't going to plan, the trio then closed their eyes, to stop the gusts, but when they opened them... four blood-red eyes stared back!

Jennifer Himan (12)
Westbourne School, Sheffield

FINDING OTTO

The ticking of her watch, *tick, tick, tick*, the echo of her footsteps. *Slap, slap*, the beating of her heart, *dum, dum*, egged her on towards the deteriorating ash planks that once would've been a door. Her quivering hand reached the deathly cold knob and turned it with a spine-rattling creak. Finally, the trembling girl gathered the nerve to step into the infinite darkness before her. Now to find Otto. Her ears strained for a whimper, her eyes for a pawprint. "Callisto, I've been waiting years," said a rasping voice as two slimy hands crushed a scream from Callisto's throat...

Bethany Rowson (12)
Westbourne School, Sheffield

THE BLACK SCHOOL

In the middle of nowhere, there is a mining village that shut down because people were going down the mine and sometimes not coming back, but if they came back they were white as chalk. The buildings fell down except for this school. This school was black as the coal that they mined there. There's a saying 'anyone who enters shall come out with no knowledge!' Imagine you're there, you walk up the steps, the front door opens, there are stairs, you walk up into the first classroom. You hear, "Say goodbye, your understanding will go, you will know nothing."

Joshua Gilbert (12)
Westbourne School, Sheffield

BURIED ALIVE

It was the dead of night, Emily was wandering through the graveyard to visit her mother's grave. She desperately wanted to be there at the stroke of midnight on the night of her mother's death. She could see there was a storm brewing high in the sky. It felt like there was a storm brewing in her stomach. She knew something disastrous was about to happen. Suddenly, she feels herself falling deeper and deeper into the ground. She hit something hard. Pain seeped through every vein in her body. Emily had the gut-wrenching feeling she was being buried alive.

Elena Larkin (12)
Westbourne School, Sheffield

THE GLOOMY VILLAGE

It was a murky Monday morning so I swiftly leaped out of bed and went to explore my grandparents' vast house, they lived in an old gloomy village in the middle of nowhere. Tentatively, I stumbled through some woods and found an abandoned house that looked haunted. The house was trembling. I entered the house, the smell was damp, like rotten wood and there were mountains of old gloomy furniture. Suddenly there was a howling sound inside the house. I was terrified, fearful, I turned back and ran for my life, my heart beating wildly. I needed sanctuary fast.

Rui Seymour (11)
Westbourne School, Sheffield

ONE EERIE NIGHT

"April? Where are you?" No response. I tensely opened the creaky wooden door to enter the abandoned eerie church. It was so dark but I took the step forward. I knew I shouldn't! The door slammed shut behind me like it was alive. I ran back to try to open it but it wouldn't budge. Out of nowhere, a deafening deep voice started to talk saying, "One, two, Coraline's coming for you, three, four get ready for the gore..." I saw the other exit waiting for me so I ran faster than I ever have before, then *boom!* It happened!

Isabella Spencer (11)
Westbourne School, Sheffield

THE ADJOINING ROOM

I checked into the nearby B&B in Whitby, which seemed very cosy, the host was extremely welcoming. I was the only visitor there. I progressed up the flight of stairs and entered my room. The room decor didn't complement the house or the host. The walls were a deep scarlet, the carpet was a smoky colour, the tables and chairs were black. The coffin-like bed was black, deep red curtains. As I laid my bags down I heard voices in the adjoining room. I thought I was the only one here I ventured next door to investigate, everything went black...

Poppy Fletcher (12)
Westbourne School, Sheffield

WHISPER

A young kid called Josh had just run away from home and crept into a ghastly, dingy forest and hid there for a few hours. He gazed around him and every direction looked the same, he strolled deeper into the woods and the forest got darker and hair-raising. In the distance, he saw a faint outline of a shed and as he got closer, the shed looked to be old and derelict. An abnormal, spine-chilling voice whispered into his ear, "Josh, Josh, Josh." He started to convulse and tremble, he felt a hand touch his left shoulder. He blacked out...

Leo Reed (12)
Westbourne School, Sheffield

THE TERROR IN THE WOODS

"Don't miss the bus or you'll have to go through the woods."
My mother's words play fresh in my mind as I enter the
thicket of gnarled trees, the atramentous night sky leering
down at me. With a deep breath, I begin the seemingly
endless walk back home. Now I'm terrified, silently creeping
through the dark. I hear a rustle above me and run.
Probably just a bird but everybody knows the story of what
happened in these woods. I can't get it out of my mind. I
glimpse a hideous figure and I know the nightmare is real.

George Blank (11)

Westbourne School, Sheffield

THE GRAVEYARD

Wandering through the graveyard feeling like something was watching me, I peered round to feel the icy fingers gripping my arm in the darkness. Running for dear life, I could feel a ghost in my body. I heard a shrill cry echoing in the mist. I knew there was something still out there. I ran into the house surprised to see the sight of my mother lying dead on the ancient floor. I walked through thick red blood which was splattered up the walls. What evil lurked in this place? What should I do next? Screaming, I saw the spectre...

Matilda White (12)
Westbourne School, Sheffield

THE COOKIE

It was a dark and stormy night, I was finishing a batch of biscuits and heard a loud shriek coming from outside. Terrifyingly there was a murder of crows flying over the body of an old woman who had been shot. Suddenly, the view blurred and the body was gone. It was a monster. I ran back inside and another loud bang. I did not know what was happening. I went to bed and then I woke up very early, a ghostly lady floated above me, ancient and corpse-like, elevated above me. The lady slowly began saying, "You did this!"

Anton Singleton (12)
Westbourne School, Sheffield

THE COTTAGE

In the dark cottage of the sinister ancient forest, a chill ran down my spine as I crept down the halls and tried to return to my camp after the rest of my patrol had gone missing. I tried to be as quiet as possible, I heard a horrible sound echo down the halls so I speeded up, the sounds of the old dilapidated floorboards were incredibly loud, I tried to be silent, it made it worse. I started jogging then I went faster, I got even faster I had broken into a sprint. Until suddenly, darkness. Hellish, dark nothingness.

Samuel Peters (12)
Westbourne School, Sheffield

THE REVENGE

It's been years, why now? It's them. I know it is and they are coming. Coming for me! This is it. This is my contribution to the world and it is all over. They must have been waiting all this time. I can't imagine anyone else who would want to kill me. I've made it to the woods, I'm nearly home! No! My phone is dead! I can't see them anymore but I know they're here. Knife in hand, I am willing to fight to the end. There is breath on the back of my neck. Oh god!

Harry Carter (12)
Westbourne School, Sheffield

THE MASK

After buying the mask on a gloomy night in the back lanes of London, Archie took it home and hid it under his bed. Now it seemed to give off a horrible chill feeling, it was green and also cold and heavy and the face was terribly frightening. The face had been so spooked by something from its expression, Archie thought it would be cool for the play, but now he was scared of it. So he took it from under the bed and tried to throw it out the window, but it came back and stuck to his face!

Harry Johnstone (12)
Westbourne School, Sheffield

THE STRANGLER

On a dark, strange night, Tom, a 14-year-old boy ran into an abandoned school to avoid the rain. But as he entered, the doors slammed shut and he was locked in. He tried to look for a way out in the classroom but when Tom looked in a certain classroom he saw bloodstains on the floor. In a state of shock, he collapsed to the floor. Then suddenly a mystery man knocked Tom out and tied him to a cliff, and woke him up. The man lifted Tom and strangled him. The man revealed himself to be...

Charlie Jackson (12)
Westbourne School, Sheffield

YOUNG WRITERS INFORMATION

We hope you have enjoyed reading this book – and that you will continue to in the coming years.

If you're a young writer who enjoys reading and creative writing, or the parent of an enthusiastic poet or story writer, visit our website **www.youngwriters.co.uk/subscribe** to join the World of Young Writers and receive news, competitions, writing challenges, tips, articles and giveaways! There is lots to keep budding writers motivated to write!

If you would like to order further copies of this book, or any of our other titles, then please give us a call or order via your online account.

Young Writers
Remus House
Coltsfoot Drive
Peterborough
PE2 9BF
(01733) 890066
info@youngwriters.co.uk

Join in the conversation!
Tips, news, giveaways and much more!

 **YoungWritersUK**    **YoungWritersCW**    **youngwriterscw**